COLLECTION 6

COLLECTION 6

Why I'm Afraid of Bees

Deep Trouble

Go Eat Worms

R.L. Stine

Hippo

Scholastic Children's Books,
Commonwealth House, 1–19 New Oxford Street, London WC1A lNU, UK
a division of Scholastic Ltd
London ~ New York ~ Toronto ~ Sydney ~ Auckland

First published in this edition by Scholastic Ltd, 1997

Why I'm Afraid of Bees
Deep Trouble
Go Eat Worms
First published in the USA by Scholastic Inc., 1994
First published in the UK by Scholastic Ltd, 1995
Copyright © Parachute Press, Inc., 1994

GOOSEBUMPS is a trademark of Parachute Press, Inc.

ISBN 0 590 19255 8

Typeset by Contour Typesetters, Southall, London
Printed by Cox & Wyman Ltd, Reading, Berks

10 9 8 7 6 5 5 3

CONTENTS

Why I'm Afraid of Bees

If you're afraid of bees, I have to warn you—there are a *lot* of bees in this story. In fact, there are hundreds.

Up until last month, I was afraid of bees. And when you read this story, you'll see why.

It all started in July when I heard a frightening *buzz*, the buzz of a bee.

I sat up straight and searched all around. But I couldn't see any bees anywhere. The scary buzzing sound just wouldn't stop. In fact, it seemed to be getting louder.

"It's probably Andretti again," I told myself. "Ruining my day, as usual."

I'd been reading a stack of comic books under the big maple tree in my back garden. Other kids might have better things to do on a hot, sticky summer afternoon—like maybe going swimming with their friends.

But not me. My name is Gary Lutz, and I have to be honest. I don't have many close friends.

3

Even my nine-year-old sister, Krissy, doesn't like me very much. My life is the pits.

"Why is that?" I constantly ask myself. "What exactly is wrong with me? Why do all the kids call me names like Lutz the Klutz? Why does everybody always make fun of me?"

Sometimes I think it might be because of the way I look. That morning, I'd spent a long time studying myself in the mirror. I'd stared at myself for at least half an hour.

I saw a long, skinny face, a medium-sized nose, and straight blond hair. Not exactly handsome, but not terrible.

Bzzzzzz.

I can't stand that sound! And it was coming even closer.

I flopped over on my stomach. Then I peered around the side of the maple tree. I wanted to get a better view of my neighbour's garden.

Oh, no, I thought. I was right. The buzzing sound was coming from Mr Andretti's bees. My neighbour was at it again. He was always hanging about by his garage, messing around with those bees of his.

How could he handle them every day without worrying about getting stung? I asked myself. Didn't they give him the creeps?

I climbed to my knees and edged a few centimetres forward. Even though I wanted to get a better look at Mr Andretti, I didn't want him to see me.

4

The last time he caught me watching him, he made a big fuss about it. He acted as if there was some kind of law against sitting outside in your own back garden!

"What's this?" he bellowed at the top of his lungs. "Did someone start a neighbourhood watch committee without informing me? Or is MI5 recruiting ten-year-old spies these days?"

This last remark really got my back up, because Mr Andretti knows perfectly well that I'm *twelve* years old. After all, my family has lived next door to him for my entire life. Which is bad luck for me. Mainly since I'm afraid of bees.

I might as well confess it right away. I'm scared of a few other things, too, such as dogs, bullies, the dark, loud noises, and swimming in the sea. I'm even scared of Claus. That's Krissy's stupid cat.

But, most of all, I'm scared of bees. Unfortunately, with a beekeeper for a neighbour, there are *always* bees around. Hairy, crawly, buzzing, stinging bees.

"*Meow!*"

I jumped up as Claus the cat came creeping up behind me. "Why do you have to startle me like that?" I cried.

As I spoke, Claus moved forward and wrapped himself around my leg. Then he dug his long, needle-sharp claws into my skin.

5

"Ouch!" I screamed. "Get away from me!" I cannot understand how Krissy can love that creature so much. She says he only jumps on me because he "likes" me. Well, all I can say is that I *don't* like him! And I wish he would keep away from me!

When I finally managed to chase Claus away, I went back to studying my neighbour. Yes, I'm scared of bees. And I'm fascinated by them, too.

I can't seem to stop watching Mr Andretti all the time. At least he keeps his hives in a screened-in area behind his garage. That makes me feel pretty safe. And he acts as if he knows what he's doing. In fact, he acts as if he's the world's greatest living expert on bees!

Today, Mr Andretti was wearing his usual bee outfit. It's a white suit, and a hat with a gauze veil hanging down to protect his face. His clothes are tied with string at the wrists and ankles. He looks just like some kind of alien creature out of a horror film.

As my neighbour carefully opened and closed the drawer-like sections of his hanging hives, I noticed he wasn't wearing any gloves.

Once, when I was with my dad, Mr Andretti had explained this to us. "It's like this, Lutz," he said. Lutz is my father, Ken Lutz. Naturally, during this entire conversation, Mr Andretti had acted as if I wasn't even there.

6

"Your average beekeepers usually wear gloves," he explained. "A lot of the brave ones use gloves with no fingers and thumbs so they can work with the bees more easily."

Mr Andretti thumped himself on the chest and went on. "But your truly outstanding bee-keeper—such as myself—likes to work with his bare hands. My bees trust me. You know, Lutz, bees are really a lot smarter than most people realize."

Oh, right, I said to myself at the time. If they're really so smart, why do they keep coming back to your hive and letting you steal all their honey from them?

Bzzzzzz.

The humming from Mr Andretti's hives suddenly grew louder and more threatening. I stood up and walked over to the fence between our two back gardens. I gazed into the screened-in area to see what was going on.

Then I gasped out loud.

Mr Andretti's white suit didn't look white any more. It had become *black*!

Why? Because he was totally *covered* with bees!

As I stared, more and more of the insects oozed out of their hives. They crawled all over Mr Andretti's arms and chest, and even on his head.

I was so freaked out, I thought I might puke!

7

Mr Andretti's hat and veil shimmered and bulged as if they were *alive*!

Wasn't he scared of all those stingers?

As I leaned over the fence, Andretti suddenly yelled at me: *"Gary—look out!"*

I froze. "Huh?"

"The bees!" Mr Andretti screamed. "They're out of control! Run!"

8

I never ran so fast in my life! I charged across the lawn and stumbled up the back steps of my house.

I flung open the screen door and almost fell into the house. Then I stopped and leaned against the kitchen table, gasping for air.

When I finally caught my breath, I listened hard. I could still hear the angry buzzing of the bees from the next garden. Then I heard something else.

"Haw haw haw!"

Somebody was laughing out there. And it sounded suspiciously like Mr Andretti.

Slowly, I turned around and peered out through the screen door. My neighbour was standing at the bottom of the back steps. He'd taken off his bee veil, and I could see that he had a huge grin on his face.

"Haw haw! You should have seen the expression on your face, Gary. You never would believe how funny you looked! And the way you *ran!*"

I stared at him. "You mean your bees weren't escaping?"

Mr Andretti slapped his knees. "Of course they weren't! I have complete control of those bees at all times. They come and go, bringing nectar and pollen back from the flowers."

He paused to wipe some sweat off his forehead. "Of course, sometimes I have to go out and recapture a few lost bees with my net. But most of them know my hives are really the best home they can possibly have!"

"So this was all a joke, Mr Andretti?" I tried to sound angry. But that's hard to do when your voice is shaking even harder than your knees! "It was supposed to be funny?"

"I hope that'll teach you to get a life and stop staring at me all day!" he replied. Then he turned and walked away.

I was so angry! What a cruel trick!

It was bad enough having kids my own age pick on me all the time. But now the grown-ups were starting it!

I pounded my fist on the kitchen table just as my mother walked into the room. "Hi, Gary," she said, frowning. "Try not to destroy the furniture, okay? I was just about to make myself a sandwich. Would you like one?"

"I suppose so," I muttered, sitting down at the table.

"Would you like the usual?"

I nodded. "The usual" was peanut butter and jam, which I never get tired of. For a snack, I usually like tortilla chips, the spicier the better. As I waited for my sandwich, I ripped open a new bag of chips and started chewing away.

"Uh-oh." Mum was rummaging through the fridge. "I'm afraid we're out of jam. I think we'll have to use something else."

She pulled out a small glass jar. "How about this with your peanut butter?"

"What is it?" I asked.

"Honey."

"Honey!" I shrieked. "*No way!*"

Later, I was feeling lonely. I wandered over to the school playground. As I walked past the swing set, I saw a bunch of kids I knew from school.

They were standing around on the baseball diamond, choosing sides for a game. I joined them. Maybe, just maybe, they'd let me play.

"Gail and I are captains," a boy named Louie was saying.

I walked over and stood at the edge of the group. I was just in time.

One by one, Louie and Gail picked players for

11

their teams. Every kid was chosen. Every kid except one, that is. I was left standing by myself next to home plate.

As I slumped my shoulders and stared down at the ground, the captains starting fighting over me. "You take him, Gail," Louie said.

"No. *You* take him."

"No way. I always get stuck with Lutz!"

As the two captains argued over who was going to be stuck with me, I could feel my face getting redder and redder. I wanted to leave. But then they all would have said I was a quitter.

Finally, Gail sighed and rolled her eyes. "Oh, all right," she said. "We'll take him. But remember the special Lutz rule. He gets *four* strikes before he's out!"

I swallowed hard and followed my teammates out on to the diamond. At that point, luck was with me. Gail sent me to the outfield.

"Go way out to the right, Lutz," Gail ordered. "By the back fence. Nobody ever hits it out there."

Some kids might be angry about being stuck so far away from the action. But I was grateful. If no balls were hit to me, I wouldn't have a chance to drop them the way I always did.

As I watched the game, my stomach slowly tied itself into a tight knot. I was last in the batting order. But when my turn at the plate finally came around, the bases were loaded.

I picked up the bat and wandered out towards the plate. A groan rose up from my teammates. "Lutz is up?" somebody cried in disbelief.

"Easy out!" yelled the girl playing first base. "No batter, no batter, no batter!" Everyone on the other team hooted and laughed. Out of the corner of my eye I saw Gail put her face in her hands.

I ground my teeth together and started praying. Please let me get a walk. Please let me get a walk. I knew I could never hit the ball. So a walk was my one and only hope.

Of course I struck out.

Four straight strikes.

"Lutz the Klutz!" I heard someone cry. Then a lot of kids laughed.

Without looking back, I marched off the baseball diamond and away from the playground. I was heading home towards the peace and quiet of my own room. It might not be perfect, I thought. But at least at home no one teased me about being a klutz.

"Hey, look guys!" a voice shouted as I turned into my street.

"Hey—wow—it's Lutz the Klutz!" someone else answered.

"Lookin' good, dude!"

I couldn't believe my bad luck. The three voices belonged to the biggest, meanest,

toughest creeps in the entire neighbourhood—
Barry, Marv, and Karl. They're my age, but at
least five times as big!

These guys are *gorillas*! I mean, their knuckles
drag on the pavement!

And when they're not swinging back and
forth on a tyre swing in their gorilla cage, what's
their favourite activity?

You guessed it. Beating me up!

"Give me a break, guys," I pleaded. "I'm
having a bad day."

They laughed.

"You want a *break*, Lutz?" one of them
shouted menacingly. "Here!"

I only had time to blink as I watched a huge,
mean-looking fist heading right for my nose.

A long, painful ten minutes later, I walked through the back door of my house. Fortunately, my mum was somewhere upstairs. She didn't see my bloody nose, scratched, bruised arms, and torn shirt.

All I needed was for her to start fussing over me and threatening to phone the other boys' parents. If that happened, Barry, Marv, and Karl really *would* kill me the next time they saw me.

As I crept up the stairs, Claus the cat came leaping out at me.

"*Yowl!*"

"Whoooooa!" I was so shocked, I almost fell back down the stairs. "Get away from me, you monster!"

I pushed the cat away and hurried into the bathroom. I gazed into the mirror and almost heaved. I looked like death warmed up.

I rinsed my nose with ice-cold water. Then I

cleaned off all the blood and staggered to my room.

I took off my ripped T-shirt and hid it behind my bed. Then I put on a winter shirt with long sleeves. It would be hot, but it would hide my scratched arms.

Downstairs in the kitchen, I found Mum and Krissy. Mum was getting out mixing bowls and eggs, and Krissy was tying a big apron around her waist. As usual, Claus was purring and wrapping himself around Krissy's legs. Why did he act like such an innocent little kitten around her, and such a monster around me?

"Hi, Gary," my mum said to me. "Do you want to help us make peanut butter cookies?"

"No, thanks," I said. "But I'll lick the bowl for you later." I walked over to the table and picked up the bag of tortilla chips I'd left there before.

"Well, at least you can help by getting that new jar of peanut butter out of the cupboard and opening it for me," Mum said. "This recipe calls for a lot of peanut butter."

"Sounds good," I said. "Just so long as it doesn't have any honey in it."

I opened the cupboard door and took out the peanut butter. I tried to twist off the cap. I twisted as hard as I could, but the top just wouldn't move. I banged the jar on the table and tried again. Still no luck.

"Do you have a wrench or something around, Mum?" I asked. "This thing just won't budge."

"Maybe if you ran hot water on it," my mother began.

"Oh, *please*!" Krissy said with a snort. Wiping her hands on her apron, she crossed the room and grabbed the jar away from me.

With two fingers, she twisted off the cap.

Then she started laughing her head off. My mum started laughing, too.

Can you believe it? My own mother was laughing at me!

"I guess you forgot to eat your Shredded Wheat this morning," Mum said.

"I'm leaving," I muttered to Mum and Krissy. "For ever."

The two of them were laughing together. I don't think they even heard me.

Totally miserable, I stepped out of the front door and slammed it hard behind me. I decided to ride my bike around for a while. When I went around to the side of the house and got it out of the garage, I started to cheer up a little bit.

My bike is really awesome. It's a new, blue, twenty-one-speed racer, and it's really sleek and cool. My dad gave it to me for my twelfth birthday.

I jumped on my bike and headed down the drive. As I turned on to the street, I saw some girls walking down the road. Out of the corner of my eye, I recognized them.

Wow! I thought. It's Judy Donner and Kaitlyn Davis!

Both Judy and Kaitlyn go to my school. They're really pretty and very popular.

To be honest, I've had a massive crush on Judy since the fourth grade. And once, at the fifth-grade picnic, she actually smiled at me. At least, I think it was at me.

So when I saw those girls walking down the street, I decided it was a good time to try to be really cool.

I flipped the baseball cap around so the brim was at the back of my head. Then I folded my arms across my chest and started pedalling no-handed.

As I passed them, I glanced over my shoulder and flashed my most glamorous smile at Judy and Kaitlyn.

Before my beautiful smile faded, I felt a tug at my trainer. I realized instantly that my shoelace was caught in the chain!

A horrible grinding sound filled the air. The bike jerked and lurched from side to side—and I lost control!

"Gary—!" I heard Judy shriek. "Gary—look out for that car!"

CRAAAAAAACK.

I didn't see the lamp-post until I hit it.

As I toppled off my bike and shot sideways through the air, I heard the sound of metal crumpling, ripping, and shredding.

I landed on my face in a deep, warm puddle of mud.

I heard the car rumble past me.

Slowly, I pulled my face out of the mud.

I reckon I didn't look too cool, I thought bitterly. Maybe at least I'll get a little sympathy.

No way.

I could hear Judy and Kaitlyn laughing behind me on the pavement. "Nice bike, Gary!" one of them called. They hurried away.

I had never been so humiliated in all my life. If I could have, I would have put down roots in that mud puddle and turned myself into a tree. It might not be the most exciting life in the world.

But at least no one laughs at a tree.

I'm serious. At that moment, I would have happily swapped lives with a tree. Or a bird. Or an insect. Or just about any other living object on the planet.

With that sad thought, I decided to get myself up and out of there before anyone else came along. It took all my strength to peel my wrecked bicycle off the lamp-post. Luckily, I didn't have far to drag it.

For the second time in the same afternoon, I crept into my house and up the stairs so I could get cleaned up before anyone saw me. Now, as I studied my reflection in the bathroom mirror, I saw there was no way I could hide all my cuts and scrapes from my mum.

"Oh, who cares?" I moaned as I washed the mud off my face and hands. "Who cares if Mum sees them? I'll be doing her a favour by giving her something *else* to laugh at. It'll really make her day!"

I went back into my room and changed into my last clean shirt. Then I glanced around, trying to find something to do.

I decided to boot up my computer. Playing with my computer is one of the few things I really like. When I'm lost in the world of a computer game, sometimes I can actually forget I'm a total fool named Gary Lutz. Nobody in a computer game ever calls me Lutz the Klutz.

I turned on the computer and decided to have another try at the *Planet Monstro* fantasy game I'd been stuck on for two days. *Monstro* is a really cool game.

When you play it, you're a character named The Warrior, and you're trapped on the planet Monstro. You have to get yourself out of all kinds of scary situations.

Before I started to play, I thought I'd check Computa Note, one of the electronic bulletin boards I'm connected to on the computer.

I'd left a message there on Monday, asking if anyone knew how to defeat the two-headed dragon that kept eating me on the thirteenth moon of Monstro. Sometimes other people in the country who are playing the same game will send each other hints.

When I accessed Computa Note, I saw the following computer-game-related messages on the screen:

To Arnold in Milwaukee: Have you tried rubbing smashed-up eucalyptus leaves all over yourself in the rainforest game? It's an ecologically correct way of repelling the poisonous ants in EcoScare 95. *From Lisa in San Francisco*

To R from Sacramento: The only way to escape from the flood on your spaceship in

21

SpaceQuest 20 is to inflate your suit and float away. *From L in St. Louis*

To Gary in Millville: Try stabbing the dragon between the eyes. It worked for me. *From Ted in Ithaca*

Oh, terrific, I thought. I'd been *trying* to stab the dragon between the eyes. But the creature always ate me before I could do it! What was "Ted in Ithaca" doing that I wasn't?

I decided to leave another electronic note, asking Ted to explain what he meant. But, as I started typing, I noticed another message at the very bottom of the computer screen.

I read it. Then I read it again very carefully:

TAKE A HOLIDAY FROM YOURSELF.
Change places with someone for a week!

What could that mean?

I pressed the Enter button so I could read what came next. I desperately wanted more information about the message. This is what I saw:

TAKE A HOLIDAY FROM YOURSELF.
Change places with someone for a week!

PERSON-TO-PERSON HOLIDAYS
113 Roach Street, Suite 2-B
or call 1-800-555-SWAP

How could it possibly work? I asked myself. How could two people change lives without getting into all kinds of trouble?

I had to admit it sounded totally crazy.

Crazy, but interesting.

I yawned and scratched the back of my head. "Ouch!" My hand grazed one of the painful bumps I'd got from Barry, Marv, and Karl.

It really hurt. But the stab of pain helped me make up my mind. I was *definitely* ready for some changes in my life.

"I don't want to spend the rest of my life getting beaten up!" I told myself. "Or crashing into lamp-posts, either! Or being the last person chosen for the team!"

I took out a piece of paper and copied the address from the screen. As I did, I realized it was only a few streets away from my school. I knew just where it was. I could pop into the Person-to-Person office the next day.

I'm really going to check it out, I decided.

Making up my mind like that improved my mood a lot. I was beginning to feel almost cheerful when I went back downstairs. But not for long. When my family sat down in the dining room for dinner, my father noticed my battered face.

"Gary!" he exclaimed. "What in the world happened to you?"

"Er," I said. "I had a little accident on my bike." I winced as I said the word "bike." I was thinking about the mangled wreck in the corner of the garage.

"I don't believe that for a minute," Mum said. "I'm sure you've been fighting with those big kids in the neighbourhood again. Why in the world can't you children learn to settle your disagreements peacefully?"

24

Krissy started laughing so hard, she almost choked on her tuna casserole. "Gary doesn't have any disagreements with those guys, Mum!" she said. "They just like to beat him up!"

My mother shook her head angrily. "Well, I think that's just outrageous!" she said. "I have a good mind to phone those boys' parents up right now and give them a piece of my mind!"

I groaned loudly. "I'm telling you, Mum, I really had an accident with my bike. If you don't believe me, go and have a look in the garage."

Then my father *did* believe me. He started lecturing me about bike safety and why I should have been wearing my helmet and how I was going to have to pay to have the bike fixed with my own money.

After a while, I stopped paying much attention. As I pushed my casserole around on my plate, all I could think about was my plan for changing my life with Person-to-Person Holidays.

The sooner the better, I thought. The sooner I get out of this life, the better off I'll be.

We finished dinner, and I went upstairs to play on my computer again. I spent the rest of the evening with my *Planet Monstro* game.

I kept trying to stab the dragon between the eyes. But even though I followed Ted from Ithaca's advice, I couldn't do it. The dragon ate me twenty-three times.

Finally, I gave up and crawled into bed. I was so wiped out, I started drifting off to sleep almost right away. I turned over and pulled the blanket up under my chin. I curled up into a ball. The toes on my right foot touched something.

"Huh?" I said out loud. "What *is* that down there?"

My heart pounded in my chest.

Slowly, I moved my toes again.

"Ohhhhhh." My blood turned into ice.

I jumped out of bed and let out a bloodcurling scream.

Frantically, I ripped the blankets off my bed. In the dim light coming in through the window, I could see the rat—fat and hairy, its red eyes gleaming at me.

I screamed again.

Then I heard laughter down the hall. Krissy's laughter.

My stomach sank. I made my way to the switch and turned on the light.

Sure enough. The rat still stared at me from my bed. But now I recognized it. A grey rubber rat. One of Claus's favourite toys.

In her room down the hall, Krissy squealed with laughter.

"I'm going to get you, you little brat!" I screamed. I thought about going down the hall and really thumping her. But I quickly decided against it.

Even though Krissy is only nine, she happens to be pretty strong. There was an excellent chance she could beat me up.

With an angry growl, I grabbed the rat off my bed and flung it into the corner of my room. Then, my heart still pounding with rage, I turned off the light and climbed back under the covers.

"Tomorrow," I promised myself in the dark room. "Tomorrow, you, Gary Lutz, are going to check out that ad and find out if you can change your life. Even if it's only for a week, it has to be better than this miserable life you have now!"

The next day I kept my promise to myself. After breakfast, I walked to Roach Street and started reading the street numbers, trying to find number 113.

I suppose I was looking for some kind of big, glass office building. But when I finally found number 113, it was on a small, grey building that looked something like my dentist's surgery. A little sign on the outside read:

PERSON-TO-PERSON HOLIDAYS
Suite 2-B

I opened the door and walked up a flight of steps. At the top, I opened another door and went into a kind of waiting room with beige carpeting and tan leather chairs.

A dark-haired woman sat behind a big glass window. She smiled at me when I came in, and I walked over to talk to her.

"Good afternoon," she said into a microphone.

I jumped. Even though the woman was right in front of me, her voice came out through a speaker on the wall.

"Uh . . . um," I stammered nervously. "I came about the message on the electronic bulletin board?"

"Oh, yes," the woman replied with another smile. "A lot of people learn about us from their computers. Pardon me for staying behind this glass shield. But the equipment behind me is so delicate, we have to be very careful about protecting it."

I peered over the woman's shoulder. I could see gleaming metal counters and a wall of electronic equipment, video screens, X-ray machines, and cameras. It looked like something right out of *Star Trek*!

I suddenly had a heavy feeling in my stomach. Maybe this is a bad idea, I thought. "Y-you probably don't like kids hanging around in here," I stammered. I started backing away towards the door.

"Not at all," she said. "Many of our customers are young people such as you. A lot of kids are interested in changing places with someone else for a week. What did you say your name was?"

"Gary. Gary Lutz."

"Nice to meet you, Gary. My name is Miss Karmen. How old are you? About twelve?"

I nodded.

"Come over here for a minute," Miss Karmen said, motioning with her hand.

Cautiously, I walked back over to the glass booth. She opened a little slot at the bottom of her window and pushed out a book. I picked it up and saw that it was a photo album, like the one my parents have from their wedding.

I opened it and started looking through it. "It's kids!" I exclaimed. "All about my age."

"Correct," said Miss Karmen. "They're all interested in swapping lives with someone else for a week."

"Wow." I studied the album.

A lot of the kids in the pictures looked big and strong. And cool. Kids like that wouldn't be afraid of anything, I told myself. I wondered what it would be like to be one of them.

"You can pick a boy—or even a girl, for that matter—to swap places with for a week," Miss Karmen was saying.

"But how does it work?" I asked. "Do I just take over somebody's room and live in his house for a week? Go to his school? Wear his clothes?"

The woman laughed. "It's far more interesting than that, Gary. With our getaway breaks, you

30

actually *become* the other person for a week."

"Huh?"

"What we have," the woman explained, "is a safe, painless way to switch one person's mind into another person's body. So, while *you'll* know you're really you, no one else will recognize you. Not even the other boy's parents!"

I was still confused. "But . . . what about my body? Does it get stored here?"

"No, no. We here at Person-to-Person will find someone else to take over your body for the week. Your parents will never even know you're gone!"

I looked down at my skinny body and wondered who could possibly want to borrow it for a week. Miss Karmen leaned forward in her chair. "So what do you say? Are you interested, Gary?"

I stared into her dark brown eyes and swallowed hard. I broke into a cold sweat. This whole thing was really weird—and *scary*! "Uh," I said. "I don't know. I mean I'm just not sure."

"Don't feel bad," Miss Karmen said. "Many people take some time to get used to the idea of a body switch. You can think it over for as long as you wish."

She took out a small camera. "But in the meantime, would you mind if I took your picture? That way, we can find out if anyone is interested in being in your body for a week."

31

"Well, I suppose so," I replied.

She took the picture, and the flash went off in front of my eyes. "But I'm still not sure I want to go through with it."

"There's no obligation," Miss Karmen said. "Why don't we leave it this way? You fill out a form describing yourself. Then I'll put your picture into our display album. And, when we find someone to take your place, I'll call you to see if you've made up your mind."

"Okay," I replied. What harm could that do? I asked myself. There was *no way* she would ever find anybody who'd want *my* body for a week!

I spent a few minutes filling out the form. I had to write down my name and address. Then I had to tell all about my hobbies, and how well I did in school, and things like that. When I had finished, I handed it to Miss Karmen, said goodbye, and headed out of the door.

I made it most of the way home without getting into trouble. A couple of roads from my house, I ran into my three most unfavourite people in the world—Barry, Marv, and Karl.

"Hey, guys!" Barry cried with an ugly smile. "The Klutz is up and walking around. That must mean we didn't do a very good job of pounding him yesterday."

"No," I insisted. "You did a good job. You did a *very* good job, guys!"

32

I suppose they didn't believe me. They all jumped me at once.

When they had finally finished—about five minutes later—I lay on the ground and watched them walk away through one swollen black eye.

"Have a nice day!" Marv called back to me. All three of them roared with laughter.

I sat up and pounded the ground with my fist.

"I'm sick of this!" I wailed. "I want to be somebody else—*anybody* else!"

Slowly and painfully, I dragged myself to my feet. "I'm doing it," I decided. "And nobody's going to stop me. Tomorrow I'm going to phone Person-to-Person Holidays. I want them to put me into somebody else's body. As soon as they can!"

I spent the next few days changing my Band-Aids and hoping the woman from Person-to-Person Holidays would call me.

At first, I ran to answer the phone every time it rang. But of course it was never for me. Usually, it was one of Krissy's silly friends, wanting to giggle and gossip.

One afternoon, I was reading a science-fiction book in my usual spot behind the big maple tree. I heard a sound, and peered around from behind the tree.

Sure enough, there was Mr Andretti walking across the lawn. He was dressed in his bee-keeping outfit. As I watched, Mr Andretti went to the screened-in area off the garage and started opening up the little doors to his beehives.

Bzzzzzz.

I covered my ears, but I couldn't shut out the loud, droning hum. How I hated that sound! It was just so frightening.

34

I shivered and decided it was time to go back inside.

As I climbed to my feet, a bullet-sized object shot right past my nose. A bee!

Were the bees escaping for real this time?

I gasped and stared over at Andretti's house. Then I almost choked. There *was* a big hole in the screen around the beekeeping area.

A *lot* of bees were flying out!

"Ow!" I cried out as a bee landed on the side of my head and buzzed loudly into my ear.

Frantically, I batted it away. Then I ran towards the house. For one wild moment, I thought about calling the police or maybe an ambulance.

But, as I slammed the back door, I heard an all-too-familiar sound. "Haw haw haw!"

Once again, Mr Andretti was laughing at me.

I pounded my fist into my other hand. Oh, how I'd like to punch that guy on the nose! I thought.

I was interrupted by the sound of the phone ringing.

"Give me a break!" I cried as I marched off to answer it. "Don't Krissy's moron friends have anything better to do than talk on the phone all day long?"

"Whaddya want?" I snarled into the mouthpiece.

"Is this Gary?" a woman's voice asked. "Gary Lutz?"

"Uh . . . yes," I answered in surprise. "I'm Gary."

"Hi, Gary. This is Miss Karmen. From Person-to-Person Holidays? Remember me?"

My heart started thumping in my chest. "Yes. I remember," I answered.

"Well, if you're still interested, we've found a match for you!"

"A match?"

"Correct," said Miss Karmen. "We've found a boy who wants to switch bodies with you for a week. Are you interested?"

I hesitated for a few seconds. But, then, as I gazed out of the back door of the kitchen, I saw a big, fat bee throwing itself against the outside of our screen door. "Haw haw!" Mr Andretti's scornful laughter boomed across the back garden.

My mouth tightened into a thin line. "Yes," I said firmly. "I'm really interested. When can we make the switch?"

"Why, we could do it now," said Miss Karmen. "If that's all right with you."

My pulse raced as I thought. My parents were both out for the afternoon, and Krissy was playing at a friend's house. The timing was perfect. I'd never get another chance like this!

"Now is great!" I exclaimed.

"Terrific, Gary. It will take me about twenty

minutes to get to your house."

"I'll be waiting."

The next twenty minutes seemed to take for ever. While I waited, I paced back and forth in the living room, wondering what my new body would be like.

What would my new parents be like? My house? My clothes? Would I actually have some friends this time?

By the time Miss Karmen arrived, I was a wreck. When the doorbell rang, my hand was sweating so much, I could barely turn the doorknob to let her in.

"Let's go into the kitchen," Ms Karmen suggested. "I like to set up my equipment on a table." She opened a small case and took out some black boxes with monitors on them.

I showed her the way to the kitchen. "So who's this kid who wants to swap places with me?" I asked.

"His name is Dirk Davis."

Dirk Davis! I thought excitedly. Even his name sounded cool. "What does he look like?"

Miss Karmen opened up a white photo album. "Here's his picture," she said, passing it to me.

I looked down at a picture of a tall, athletic-looking blond boy in black Lycra cycling shorts and a blue muscle shirt. I blinked in surprise.

"He looks like a surfer or something!" I cried. "Why in the world does he want to swap bodies with me? Is this some kind of trick?"

Miss Karmen smiled. "Well, to be honest, it's not exactly your *body* he's interested in, Gary. He wants your *mind*. You see, Dirk needs someone who is good at maths. He has some very hard maths tests coming up in summer school. He wants you to take them for him."

"Oh," I said. I felt relieved. "Well, I usually do pretty well in maths tests."

"We know that, Gary. Person-to-Person does its homework. You're very good at maths. Dirk's good at skateboarding."

I sat down at the table.

Bzzzzzz.

A bee buzzed right under my nose. "Hey!" I yelled, jumping back up. "How'd that bee get in here?"

Miss Karmen glanced up from her equipment. "Your back door is open just a bit. Now please sit down and try to relax. I need to fasten this strap around your wrist."

With a nervous glance at the back door, I sat back down. Miss Karmen strapped a black band around my wrist. Then she started fiddling with some wires attached to one of her machines.

Bzzzzzz.

Another bee flew in front of me, and I wriggled around in my chair.

"Please sit still, Gary. Otherwise the equipment won't work."

"Who can sit still with all these bees buzzing around in here?" I asked. I lowered my eyes and saw three fat bees walking across the table.

Bzzzzz.

Another bee flew past my right eye.

"What's up with these bees?" I was starting to panic.

"Don't pay any attention to them," Miss Karmen said, "and they won't bother you." She made one more adjustment to her machine. "Besides, Dirk Davis isn't afraid of bees. And, as soon as I flip this switch, you won't be, either!"

"But . . .!"

ZZAAAAPPPP!

A blinding white light flashed in front of my eyes.

I tried to cry out.

But my breath caught in my throat.

The light grew brighter, brighter.

And then I sank into a deep pool of blackness.

Something was wrong.

Colours returned. But they were a total blur.

I struggled to make everything come clear. But I couldn't seem to focus on anything.

My new body didn't feel right, either. I was lying on my back, and I felt as light as a feather, light enough to float away.

Could this be Dirk Davis's tall, muscular body? It certainly didn't feel like it!

Was this some kind of trick? I asked myself. Was the picture of Dirk Davis a fake? Was he really a lot smaller than he looked in the photo album?

I reached out one of my hands and tried to touch my stomach. But my hand felt really weird, too. It was small, and my arm seemed to be bending in several places at once!

What's going on? I wondered, trembling with fright.

Why do I feel so *weird*?

"Whooooa!" I cried out as I finally managed to touch my body. "Yuck." My skin was soft. And it was covered with a fine layer of fuzz.

"Help! Miss Karmen! Help! Something's wrong!" I tried to shout.

But there was something wrong with my voice. It came out all tiny and squeaky. Little mouse squeaks.

I rolled over on to my stomach and tried to get up. I spread my arms to balance myself.

I gasped as I realized my feet weren't even touching the ground!

I was flying!

"What's happening to me?" I cried in my squeaky little voice. I floated forward and crashed into a kitchen cupboard.

"Ow! Help me!"

I moved my strange new arms and realized I had some control over which way I flew. I felt some weird muscles in my back going into action. Testing my new muscles, I flew over to the kitchen window.

Exhausted, I landed on the sill. I turned my head to one side. Then I gasped in fright.

A hideous monster was reflected in the window glass!

The creature had two huge glaring eyes. And it was staring right at me.

I tried to scream. But I was too terrified to utter a sound.

I—I have to get away! I decided.

I moved my feet and started to run. The monster in the glass ran, too.

I stopped and stared at the window glass. The monster stopped and stared back at me.

"Oh, no! Please—no!" I cried. "Please don't let it be true!" I reached up and tried to cover my eyes. The creature in the window did the same thing.

And suddenly I knew the hideous truth. The monster in the mirror—it was me.

Miss Karmen had messed up. Totally.

And now I was trapped inside the body of a bee!

I don't know how long I stood there.

I couldn't stop staring at my reflection.

I kept waiting to come out of this nightmare. I kept waiting to blink my eyes and find myself in Dirk Davis's big, muscular body.

But I didn't look at all like Dirk Davis.

I had two giant eyes—one on either side of my head—and two skinny little antennae sticking out of my forehead.

My mouth was truly disgusting. I had some kind of long tongue, which I soon discovered I could move all around and make longer and shorter if I wanted. Which I didn't.

My body was covered with thick, black hair. I had three legs on either side of my body. And let's not forget the wings sticking out of my shoulders!

"This is the pits!" I cried. "I'm an insect! I'm a disgusting, hairy insect! Miss Karmen— something went wrong! *Help me!*"

43

Creeeeak.

Slam.

What was that?

Oh, no! I realized that Miss Karmen had just gone out of the kitchen door.

"No—wait! Wait!" I squeaked. She was my only hope!

I had to catch her. I had to tell her what had happened!

"Miss Karmen!" I squeaked. "Miss Karmen!"

Frantically, I flew out of the kitchen into the living room. Out of the window, I could see her car still parked in front of the house.

But the front door to the outside was shut. And bees can't open doors. I was trapped inside my own house!

The back door! I remembered. Miss Karmen had said it was open just a bit.

Yes! That was how all those bees got into the house in the first place!

I fluttered my new wings and flew back into the kitchen. As I soared, I realized I was getting more and more control over my flight pattern.

But I didn't care about that right now. All I knew was that I *had* to get to Miss Karmen before she drove away.

I darted out through the tiny opening in the back door. "Miss Karmen!" I shouted as I flew around the side of the house. "Miss Karmen! Help me! You messed up! I'm a bee. Help me!"

My voice was so tiny, she couldn't hear me. She opened the car door and started to climb behind the wheel. My only chance for a normal life was about to drive away!

What could I do? How could I get her attention?

Thinking quickly, I flew right towards her head. "Miss Karmen!" I shouted in her ear. "It's me. Gary!"

Miss Karmen uttered a startled cry. Then she drew back her hand and swatted me. Hard.

"Ow!" My entire body vibrated with pain. The force of her swat sent me falling to the street. I hit the pavement with a painful *splat*.

I shook my head, trying to clear my eyes. That's when I realized I had an extra set of tiny eyes arranged in a kind of triangle on the top of my head. I used them to gaze straight up.

And then I screamed in terror.

I saw the tyre rolling towards me.

Miss Karmen was about to drive right over me. I was about to be squashed like the insect that I was!

"Oh!" I froze in panic.

Even with my blurred bee vision, I could see the deep treads in the tyre as it rolled steadily towards me.

Closer. Closer.

I have to move! I told myself.

Fly away! Fly away!

But in my panic, I forgot how to use my new muscles.

I—I'm going to be squashed! I realized.

I uttered a final, weak cry.

And the car stopped.

"Huh?" My entire body was trembling. But somehow I managed to pull myself up. Up into the air.

Yes. I was flying now.

I could see Miss Karmen inside the car. She was fastening her seat belt. She had stopped the car to put on her seat belt!

"Hey, seat belts really *do* save lives!" I told myself.

I called out to her. But of course she couldn't hear me. I watched the car roll away until it was a blur of colour.

Then, exhausted and terrified, I buzzed over to a nearby lilac bush and dropped on to a leaf. "That was too close!" I told myself, in between gasps for air. "I'm going to get killed out here!"

A green caterpillar inched its way up on to a nearby stem and started chewing noisily on the leaf I was resting on. I'd never really examined a caterpillar before. Up close, they're really ugly. They look a little bit like dragons. Only scarier.

"Keep away from me!" I yelled in my tiny voice. The caterpillar didn't even turn its head. Maybe it didn't hear me.

I forgot all about the caterpillar when I heard footsteps coming up the front path. I turned my head and used my sideways eye to see who it was.

"Mum!" I screamed. "Mum! Over here!"

She couldn't hear me. She hurried up the steps and into the house.

Suddenly, I was overcome by a wave of sadness. My own mother didn't recognize me!

Desperately, I fluttered my wings and flew away from the leaf. I made my way to the front of

47

the house, and started buzzing around the front windows.

I had my wings under complete control by now. But the scene I saw inside the house was enough to make me fall down onto the ground again.

My mother stood in the living room talking to *me*! Or at least, that's what she thought. Only I knew it couldn't be me. *I* was stuck outside. But who *was* in there with my mum? Had Dirk Davis managed to get inside my body?

I landed on the ledge and stared into the house. My mum was talking. The boy was nodding and laughing. He said something to her. If I stared closely, I could read his lips.

"Hey, did you buy tortilla chips? I'm really starving, Mum."

That had to be Dirk talking inside my body.

My mum smiled at him and patted him on the arm. I read his lips and saw that he was calling her "Mum" again. How could he do that? How could he call *my* mother "Mum"?

If bees could cry—which I now know they can't—I would have started bawling right then and there. Who did that boy think he was? For that matter, what kind of mum did I have, who couldn't even tell that a total stranger was living inside her son's body?

As I watched "myself" and my mum chatting in the living room, I totally lost it. Like a crazed maniac, I started bashing my insect body into the window.

"Buzz!" I cried. "Buzz! Buzz! Buzz! It's me, Gary. Look out here! Help me!"

Again and again, I smashed myself up against the glass. But no one inside the house noticed.

After a few minutes, Mum brought the new me a bag of tortilla chips. I watched "Gary" rip the bag open and take out a handful of chips. Crumbs fell on the living room carpet as he crunched the spicy chips.

I realized I was starving.

But what do bees eat? I asked myself. Desperately, I tried to remember everything I'd ever read about the creatures.

I thought of the hungry caterpillar, crunching away on the leaf. But I was almost positive bees didn't eat leaves.

But what *did* they eat? Other insects? Ugh! The thought made me shudder. I'd *die* before I'd eat an insect.

I buzzed around the garden, hoping to see something—anything—I could use for food. As I flew, I found that I was getting used to my strange new vision and learning how to work my different sets of eyes.

I remembered something I'd once read in an old picture book called *The Big Book of Bees*. It said that bee eyes each have thousands of tiny lenses crowded together. But, because they don't have pupils, they can't really focus their eyes.

Interesting, I thought. But not very helpful. If I could remember about bees' eyesight, why couldn't I remember what they ate?

I settled on to another bush to think. And suddenly, I became aware of a wonderful odour nearby. I turned my head and saw a beautiful yellow flower.

Then I remembered something else I'd read. "Pollen," I said out loud. "Bees eat pollen. And they get it from flowers!"

Excitedly, I flew up into the air and started hovering over the yellow blossom. I tried to open my mouth—before I remembered I didn't have that kind of mouth any more!

Instead, I had my long, weird tongue. But how was I supposed to use it to get the stuff out of the flower?

I didn't have a clue!

As I hummed around in the air, I realized I was becoming more and more exhausted. If I didn't get something to eat soon, I was going to faint.

I started to feel dizzy. I hardly knew where I was.

I became more and more confused. My brain got so fuzzy, I even began to wonder if I'd ever actually been a boy at all. Maybe I'd really been a bee for my entire life, and I'd just dreamed about being a boy.

Slam!

Somebody closed a car door nearby, and I was startled out of my mental fog. I swivelled my head to look.

Dad!

He was closing the garage door. Now he was walking across the drive and heading towards the back door of the house.

"Dad!" I screamed. "Dad. It's me. Gary! Help me!"

"Hi, Gary," Dad said.

"Dad! You can hear me!" I cried joyfully. "Dad—you've got to help me!"

My heart sank when Dad walked right past me and started talking to the fake Gary.

Desperately, I started buzzing round and round their heads.

"Looks like Andretti's lost one of his workers," my dad laughed. He swatted at me with his rolled-up newspaper.

A near miss. I darted away.

"Uh, right," the fake Gary laughed, pretending he knew what Dad was talking about. "Andretti."

"Let's help get dinner on," my dad said. He put a friendly hand on my former shoulder. "Okay, son?"

"Sure thing, Dad."

Like best pals, my dad and his false son crossed the lawn and opened the screen door.

"Wait!" I shouted. "Wait!"

Like a space rocket, I shot through the air after them. If I really put the speed on, I thought I could make it through the door before it closed. Fast, faster, and . . .

BLAM!

The screen door banged shut, right on top of my tiny bee body. Once again, I sank into a deep pool of blackness.

"Ohhhhhh. Where am I? What happened? Am I still a bee?"

Dazed, I fought my way back to the real world. When I was able to get my eyes open, I realized I *was* still a bee—a small, frail, slightly damaged bee—who'd just narrowly missed being scrunched by a screen door.

Now I was lying on my back on the grass in our garden. My six legs were thrashing the air.

"I was a klutz as a human—and I'm a klutz as a bee!" I wailed. I tried to flip myself over. "I've only been a bee for an hour, and I've almost been killed. Twice!"

I suddenly knew what I had to do. I had to get to Miss Karmen's office and tell her what had happened.

I didn't know if I could do it. But I knew I had to try.

I let out a small grunt, and with a huge effort, flipped over on to my stomach. Using all five of my eyes, I checked myself out. Both sets of wings seemed to be working. And all my six legs were still there.

"Okay," I told myself. "You can do it. Just fly to the Person-to-Person office and go inside."

I flapped my wings and started to take off into the air. But I'd only risen about a centimetre up off the ground when I heard a sound that made my blood run cold.

It was Claus the cat. With his long, sharp claws extended, he leaped through the air.

I let out a squeal as he pounced on me, grabbed me in one paw, and began to tighten his claws around my body.

As the cat's claws closed around me, I saw his hideous mouth gape open.

Sting him! Sting him!

The thought burned into my mind.

But something held me back. Something told me not to use my stinger.

I suddenly remembered something else I'd read in *The Big Book of Bees*. Bumble bees die once they use their stingers!

No way! I thought.

I was still hoping to come out of this alive. And back in my old body.

So, if using my stinger was out, I'd have to use my wits instead.

With a loud gnashing of his teeth, Claus snapped his huge mouth shut. He lowered his head, preparing to snap up his furry prize—me.

At just the right moment, I burst out of his claws and ducked out from under his gnashing teeth.

I tried to shoot off through the air. But the cat whipped out his paw and batted me down.

Claus was playing with me as if I were one of the chewed-up catnip mouse toys Krissy always gives him for Christmas.

With my last burst of strength, I spread my wings, shot up through the air, and flew as fast as I could. A backwards look out of one of my eyes told me that I'd left the surprised cat sitting in the grass.

For one second, I experienced a wonderful sensation of triumph. "You did it, Gary!" I crowed to myself. "You, a tiny little bee, managed to fight off a great big vicious cat!"

I was so pleased with myself, I decided to take a little victory lap. I spread my wings out wide and began a big, slow circle in the air.

Whap!

Oh, no! Now what?

I'd crashed right into something! But what was it? It wasn't hard, like a wall or a tree. Instead, it was soft and clinging, like cloth. And my feet were all tangled up in it.

I struggled to squirm free. I wriggled and pushed. But my legs were caught.

I was trapped.

"Haw haw haw!"

The booming laughter made my entire body shake.

I suddenly realized where I was.

I was caught in Andretti's net.

A wave of despair made me slump against the white netting.

I knew exactly what would happen next.

He would put me in his hives—and I would never get away.

"Time to go back home now, my little buzzing babies," Mr Andretti sang. "Time to get back to work, my honeys." He started to laugh at his stupid pun. "My honeys! Haw haw! Oh, my, wasn't that a good one?"

Bzzzzz. Bzzzzzz.

From the loud humming sounds in my ears, I knew I wasn't the only bee Andretti had caught in his net. In fact, out of my right eye, I could see another bee who looked just like me. He loomed right in front of me, and wriggled his antennae in my face.

Whoa! What a monster!

My wiry legs began trembling with fright. I twisted myself around and around, struggling to get away from him.

I finally got myself turned the other way. But then I saw I was facing another bee. And another. Each one looked scarier than the last.

They all had big, bulging eyes and creepy

antennae! And they all buzzed menacingly at me.

The frightening hum grew louder and louder as Mr Andretti caught more bees in the net. Suddenly, the net began to shake. Up and down, up and down—like a violent earthquake—until I couldn't even think straight!

As the net shook, I lost my footing and fell into a big, squirming cluster of bees at the bottom of the net.

Whooooa! I stumbled over the pile of wriggling, hairy bees. And as I staggered in terror, bees fell on top of me.

A crawling, buzzing nightmare!

I've never been so terrified. I screamed in my tiny voice. I tried to climb up the side of the net, but my feet were stuck under another bee's body. How I hated the feel of his disgusting fuzz!

In my terror, I knew I had to escape. I had to get away from here. I had to get to Miss Karmen's office and beg her to help me.

Then I had the most terrifying thought of all. If I couldn't escape, I suddenly realized, I would remain a bee for the rest of my life!

As Mr Andretti carried me and the other bees across his back garden, I started buzzing and shivering with panic. How could this have happened to me? I asked myself. How could I ever have been so stupid as to try to change bodies with somebody else? Why wasn't I happy with the perfectly good body I'd already had?

Mr Andretti opened the door to the screened-in area off the side of his garage. "We're back now, my little honeys," he cooed.

The net started to shake, and I realized that Mr Andretti was slowly turning it inside out. One by one, he started plucking us—his prisoners—off the side of the mesh cloth and plopping each one back inside his hanging drawer hives.

As Andretti reached for the bees, they started buzzing louder than ever. Finally, it was my turn to be plucked out of the net.

When I saw the ends of Andretti's grasping fingers reaching for me, I hung back, clinging to the net. I suddenly remembered his bragging speech about how he never used gloves because his bees "trusted" him.

I watched his fingers stretch towards me.

It would be so *cool* to plunge my stinger into his soft, plump skin, I thought.

Should I do it?

Should I sting him?

Should I?

I didn't sting him.

I really didn't want to die.

Okay, things really looked terrible for me right now. But I was still clinging to a shred of hope.

Maybe, somehow, I'd find my way out of this bee prison and back into my own body. It didn't seem very likely. But I was determined to keep on trying.

"In you go, my fuzzy little friend," Mr Andretti said. He opened up one of the removable drawer-like parts of his hive and dropped me in.

"Ohhhh," I moaned. It was so dark inside the hive. And so confusing.

Where should I go? What should I do?

The air was hot and wet. Everywhere I turned, I was surrounded by a deafening, droning hum.

"I—I can't *stand* it!" I cried. I could feel myself totally losing it!

All around me, bees scurried around in the darkness. I stayed where I was, too frightened to move.

I suddenly realized I was still very hungry. If I didn't get something to eat, I knew I'd never be able to find a way out of here!

I spun around and started trying to explore.

Out of my left eye, I saw another bee glaring at me. I froze in my tracks. Did bees attack each other inside their hives? I wondered.

I didn't remember reading anything about that in my bee book. But this bee really looked ready for a fight.

"Please leave me alone," I begged in my tiny voice. "Please give me a break."

The bee glared back at me. I've never seen such big, angry-looking eyes!

Slowly, I started backing away from him. "Uh . . ." I squeaked nervously. "I've got to be going now. I . . . um . . . I have to get to work."

The bee bulged his eyes and waved his antennae in a threatening way. I was sure he planned to sting me. I turned and flew away as fast as I could. I tried to hide.

I was so frightened, I couldn't even make myself move. What if I bumped into another bee? I couldn't even stand to think about what might happen if I did.

I realized I had to move. I had to find something to eat.

Shaking with fear, I tiptoed out into the open. I took a nervous look around.

On the far wall, I could see a large cluster of bees, busily building something. A honeycomb!

And where there was a honeycomb, I told myself, there was honey.

I've always hated the sweet, sticky goo. But I knew I had to eat some. Right away!

As quietly as I could, I crept over and joined the bee workers. Out of the corner of my eye, I saw them doing really gross things with their mouths.

First, they used their legs to pick little flakes of waxy-looking stuff off their abdomens. Then they crammed the wax into their mouths and started working their jaws up and down like little chewing machines. Finally, they spat out the wax and used it to build part of the honeycomb they were working on.

"Yuck!" It looked so disgusting. It made me sick!

But what choice did I have? I had to eat some honey—even if it was covered with bee spit.

I turned my head and practised sucking my tongue up and down. Then I slurped up a big puddle of honey.

Amazing! For the first time in my life, I actually liked that stuff. Soon, I was sucking it down as if it were chocolate milk.

After a while, I got quite good with my tongue, which was actually more of a bendable tube than a tongue. It was really the perfect tool for guzzling honey.

If I ever made it back to the outside world, I thought I'd now be pretty good at using it for gathering nectar and pollen. Why, I might turn out to be the best worker in the whole hive!

I tried to smile, and then I almost gagged on my honey.

What was happening to me?

What was I thinking? I was actually starting to feel like a bee!

I *had* to get out of this place. Before it was too late!

I wanted to start searching for an escape route right away. But I suddenly felt so tired. So completely worn out . . .

Was it the honey? Or was it the strain of so much fear?

I could barely keep my eyes open. The droning hum grew louder.

With a weary sigh, I sank against a clump of hairy bodies.

I sank into the warm darkness of the hive, surrounded by the steady buzz. Breathing the sweet aroma of the honey, I sank beside my furry brothers and sisters.

I'm one of them now, I told myself weakly. I'm not a boy any more. I'm a bee. A buzzzzzzzzing bee. A bee sinking into the warm, dark hive. My home.

Sinking . . . sinking . . .

I woke up with a start and tried to brush a bee away from my face. It took me a few moments to remember. I wasn't lying in my back garden any more, trying to keep the bees away from me. I was a bee—a bee trapped inside a hive!

I jumped up, took a step, and immediately came face to face with another bee! I couldn't tell if he was the same one I'd seen the night before. But he looked just as angry. His big eyes were bulging with rage. And he was moving deliberately towards me.

As fast as I could, I spun around and flew away. Of course, I had no idea where I was going.

The hive seemed to be made up of a lot of long, dark corridors. All around me, groups of bees were building honeycombs. As they worked, they kept up a steady buzz. The sound was really driving me up the wall!

I began searching for a way out. I wandered in and out, in and out throughout the dark, sticky honeycombs.

From time to time, I shot out my tongue and lapped up some honey. I was getting a little tired of the sweet stuff. But I knew I had to keep up my strength if I wanted to try to break out of the hive.

As I searched for a way to escape, I noticed that every single bee seemed to have an assigned job, either building honeycombs, caring for the babies of the queen or whatever. And they never stopped working! They were "busy as bees" from morning till night.

Darting through the tangled darkness, I began to lose hope.

There's no way out, I decided. No way out.

I sank unhappily to the sticky hive floor. And as I dropped, three large bees moved in front of me.

They buzzed angrily, bumping up against me with their hairy, damp bodies. It was easy to tell these bees were angry with me.

Maybe it was because I wasn't doing my "job". But what *was* my job? How could I tell the boss I didn't know what I was supposed to be doing?

I tried to slip past them, but they moved to block my path.

Three tough bees. They made me think of Barry, Marv, and Karl.

I shrank back as one of them pointed his stinger at me.

He was getting ready to kill me! And I didn't even know what I'd done!

I screamed and whirled around. As fast as my six legs would carry me, I darted back down the narrow passageway and turned another corner.

"Oh!" I bumped hard into another bee. Luckily, he was hurrying off somewhere, and barely seemed to notice me.

I gasped with relief. And then the idea came to me. Where was that bee going in such a hurry? Was he taking something somewhere? Could he be going to an area I hadn't searched yet?

I decided to follow him and find out. I needed to learn everything I could about the hive. Maybe, just maybe, it would help me escape.

I hurried after the bee. I thought I'd find him quickly. But he was already long gone.

I searched in and out among the different honeycombs, but I couldn't find him anywhere. After a while, I gave up.

Nice one, Lutz the Klutz, I scolded myself. I felt worse than ever.

I shot out my tongue and slurped up a big helping of honey to keep myself going. Then I began my endless searching again.

"Whoooa!" I stopped when I reached an area that looked familiar. I was pretty sure it was the place where Andretti had dropped me when he first put me into the hive.

All at once, a large group of angrily buzzing bees crowded against me.

"Hey—!" I protested as they shoved me forward.

They replied with a sharp, rising buzz.

What were they doing? Were they attacking me? Were they all going to sting me at once?

They had me surrounded. I couldn't run away.

But how could I possibly fight off all these bees? I was doomed, I realized. Finished. Sighing in defeat, I closed my eyes and started to shake.

And waited for them to swarm over me.

I waited to be crushed.

And waited.

When I opened my eyes, the angry bees had moved to the side of the hive. They weren't paying any attention to me.

I saw a single bee, standing in the centre of the hive floor. He was performing a kind of jumping, twisting, hip-hop dance.

How weird! I thought. The other bees were watching intently, as if this were the most interesting thing in the world.

"Those bees didn't care about me," I told myself. "They were trying to get me out of the way so this bee could do his dance."

I realized I'd wasted a lot of time. I had to keep searching for an escape route.

I tried to push myself away from the group of bees, but the hive floor had become too crowded to move.

The bee danced faster and faster. He moved

his body towards the right. All the other bees stared intently at him.

What was going on?

At that moment, something from my old *Big Book of Bees* came back to me. I remembered that bees send out scouts to find their food. Then the scouts "dance" to tell the other bees where to go for it!

If the scout was reporting on where to get food, it meant he'd just been out of the hive. That meant there had to be a way out of this place!

I was so excited, *I* almost started dancing!

But I didn't have a chance because, suddenly, all the bees in the hive rose up like a dark cloud. I spread my wings and flew up with them.

As I followed, the bees formed a single, orderly line and shot out through a tiny hole in a far, upper corner of the hive.

I buzzed around until I found the end of the line. Then I got ready to escape.

Would I make it?

The very last bee in line, I shot out of the tiny hole into the open space. For a few seconds, I watched the other bees floating away, busily hunting for nectar and pollen.

I knew I looked just like them. The difference was that they would willingly return to Andretti's hive. But I never, ever would. At least, not if I could help it.

71

"I'm out!" I cried joyfully in my tiny voice. "I'm out! I'm free!"

Dazzled by the sudden bright light out of the outer world, I flew around and around in the beekeeping area. Then I headed for the hole I'd seen in the screen when I was still in my own body.

I knew it was on the wall that faced my family's garden. But when I flew over to it, I stopped and gasped in disappointment.

The hole had been patched up. Mr Andretti had fixed it!

"Oh, no!" I wailed. "I can't be trapped! I *can't* be!"

My heart started thumping crazily. My whole body was vibrating.

I forced myself to calm down and look around.

None of the other bees were in the screened-in area any more. They'd already gone outside to collect pollen. And that meant there had to be another way out.

I wasn't thinking clearly because I was exhausted, worn out from all my flying around. I sat down on top of the hive to rest.

At that instant, the door between the bee-keeping area and the garage opened. "Good morning, my little bee friend," Mr Andretti's voice boomed. "What are you doing, lying around on top of the hive? Why aren't you busy inside making me some honey? Are you sick?

You know we can't have any sick bees around here."

As I gazed up weakly, Mr Andretti moved closer. His huge, dark shadow fell over me.

I tried to curl up into a ball and disappear. But it was no use. His large fingers were stretching right towards me!

I yelled in terror. But of course, he couldn't hear me. What is he going to do to me? I asked myself. What does he *do* with sick bees?

What does he do with sick bees? I wondered again, quivering in terror.

He probably throws them in the bin, I thought. Or even worse—he feeds them to his pet bird or frog.

Despite my weariness, I knew I couldn't wait around to find out. I had to get out of there!

Just as Mr Andretti's fingers were about to fold around me, I shot up into the air and buzzed around his head. At the same instant, I saw some other bees flying in through a tiny hole in the screen. It was in the corner, near the ceiling.

I buzzed around Mr Andretti's face one more time. Then I raced towards the hole. As I tried to squeeze myself out of the exit hole, I crashed right into another bee who was flying in. He glared at me and gave me an angry buzz.

Frightened, I backed off and clung to the

screen. I had to wait for a long line of bees to come back inside. It seemed to take them for ever.

When I was finally sure the last bee had come in, I leaped forward and shot out of the hole. I was out in the open sky!

"This time I really *am* free!" I screamed in celebration, forgetting my weariness. "And Andretti's never going to catch this bee again!"

I landed on a leaf and let the morning sun warm my back and wings. It was a beautiful day—a beautiful day for finding somebody who could help me get back into my human body!

Like a rocket, I shot straight up into the air and gazed around. I recognized the familiar creak of my father opening the back door of my house.

Panting hard, I raced forward.

My father called, "Goodbye, hon! Tell the kids I'll see them tonight!" over his shoulder and let go of the door.

I darted into the house. The door slammed hard. Another near miss.

I hummed with happiness. It felt so good to be back in my own house and out of the dark, sticky hive! I landed on the counter and gazed around at the old, familiar walls.

Why hadn't I ever realized how nice my house was before?

Step, step, step.

Someone was coming into the kitchen! I flew on to the window-sill for a better look.

Krissy!

Maybe I could get her to listen to me.

"Krissy! Krissy!" I buzzed. "Over here by the window. It's me, Gary!"

To my delight, she turned and stared in my direction.

"Yes!" I cried excitedly. "Yes—it's me! It's me!"

"Oh, terrific," Krissy groaned. "One of Andretti's stupid bees has got in here again."

Okay, so it wasn't exactly the reaction I'd been hoping for. But she'd still noticed me! Maybe, I thought, if I flew right on to her shoulder and spoke into her ear, she'd be able to understand me!

My heart vibrating my entire body, I lifted myself up off the windowsill and soared towards my sister. "Krissy!" I buzzed as I approached her shoulder. "You have to listen to me!"

"Aaaaiii!"

Krissy screeched so loud, I was afraid the glass in the windows would shatter. "Get away from me, bee!"

She started thrashing her hands in the air, trying to bat me away.

"Ow!" I cried out as she slapped me. Stung with pain, I lost control and landed with a thud on the tiled worktop.

I raised my eyes in time to see Krissy grab a flyswatter out of the broom cupboard.

"No, Krissy, no!" I screamed. "Not that! You don't want to do that to your own brother!"

My sister lifted up the flyswatter and thwacked it down right next to me. I could feel the rush of air from it. And I felt the entire counter shake.

I screamed and quickly rolled to one side.

Krissy, I knew, was a menace with a flyswatter.

She was the champion in our family. She never missed.

The eyes on top of my head spun in terror. And in the grey blur, I could see the shape of the flyswatter, rising up to slap me again. And again.

18

"Stop, Krissy!" I screamed. "Stop! You're squashing me!"

With a strangled gasp, I toppled off the counter. I hit the floor hard and struggled dizzily to my feet.

Now I started to get angry. Why did Krissy have to be so bloodthirsty? Couldn't she just open a window and shoo me out?

Buzzing weakly, I floated up off the floor. Regaining my strength, I began darting wildly around the room, crashing into the walls and cupboards to show Krissy how upset I was. Then I shot out of the kitchen.

In a rage, I headed up the stairs to my room. If my sister wouldn't help me, I'd get someone else to help. Namely, the new Gary!

The morning sun was high in the sky. But "Gary" was still sound asleep in *my* bed.

Seeing him lying there so peacefully, so completely at home, made me even angrier.

78

"Wake up, you slug!" I buzzed at him. He didn't move. His mouth hung open as he slept, making him look like a real slob.

"Yuck! What a creep!" I was sure my mouth never hung open when *I* slept!

I decided to take action. I landed on "Gary's" head and started walking around on his face. I was sure my little insect legs would tickle him and wake him up.

Nothing. He didn't move.

Even when I stuck a leg up his nose, "Gary" slept without stirring.

"Why is he so tired?" I wondered. "Has he been wearing out my body?"

Furious, I ran across "Gary's" face and climbed down through his hair. Then I crawled on to his ear. "BUZZ!" I shouted as loudly as I could. "BUZZ! BUZZ! BUZZ!"

Incredible as it seems, the new "Gary" didn't even budge.

Just my luck. Dirk Davis was turning out to be the world's soundest sleeper!

I sighed and gave up. I crawled off "Gary's" ear and flew around my old room, gazing down at my bed, my dresser, and my computer.

"My computer!" I cried excitedly. "Maybe I can put a message on the screen! Maybe I can tell my parents what has happened to me!"

I swooped down to the computer, buzzing eagerly.

Yes! The computer had been left on.

What luck! I knew I wasn't heavy enough to push the Power button.

Would I be strong enough to type?

A clear blue screen greeted me on the monitor. My heart pounding, I lowered myself to the keyboard and started hopping around on the letters.

Yes! I was heavy enough to make the keys go up and down.

I paused, resting on the Enter key.

What should I type? What message should I put on the screen?

What? What? What?

As I thought frantically, I heard "Gary" stir behind me on the bed. He let out a groan. He was waking up.

Quick! I told myself. Type something! Type *anything*!

He'll see it as soon as he gets out of bed.

I hopped over to the letters and began to jump up and down, spelling out my desperate message.

It was hard work. My bee eyes weren't made for reading letters. And I kept leaping up and falling into the cracks between the keys.

After eight or nine jumps, I was gasping for air.

80

But I finished my message just as "Gary" sat up in bed and stretched.

Floating up in front of the monitor, I struggled to read what I had typed:

I AM NOT BEE. I AM GARY. HELO ME.

Through my blurred vision, I saw that I had missed the P in HELP and hit the O instead. I wanted to go back and fix it. But I was totally wiped out. I could hardly buzz.

Would they understand?

Would they read the message and see me standing on top of. the monitor and understand?

"Gary" would understand. I knew he would. Dirk Davis would work it out.

I climbed wearily to the top of the monitor and watched him climb out of bed.

Here he comes, I saw eagerly. He brushed his hair out of his eyes. He yawned. He stretched again.

Over here! I urged.

Dirk—please—look at the computer monitor!

Dirk—over here!

He picked up a crumpled pair of jeans off the floor and pulled them on. Then he found a wrinkled T-shirt to go with them.

Come on, Dirk! I pleaded, hopping up and down on top of the monitor. *Read the screen—please?*

Would he read it?

Yes! Rubbing his eyes, "Gary" shuffled over to the computer.

Yes! Yes!

I nearly burst for joy as I watched him squint at the screen. "Go ahead, Gary! Read it! Read it!" I squeaked.

He squinted at the screen some more, frowning. "Did I leave that thing on overnight?" he muttered, shaking his head. "Wow. I must be losing it."

He reached down and clicked off the power. Then he turned and made his way out of the room.

Stunned, I toppled off the monitor, landing hard on the desk beside the keyboard. All that work for nothing.

What was "Gary's" problem, anyway? Doesn't he know how to read?

I've got to talk to him, I told myself, pulling

myself together. I've got to communicate with him somehow.

I lifted my wings and floated up after him. I followed him through the kitchen, and then slipped through the back door with him.

As he strode across the grass, I started buzzing around his head. But he didn't pay any attention to me.

He crossed the lawn and opened our garage door. Then he went inside and brought out my old skateboard.

I hadn't used that skateboard in at least two years. My uncle had given it to me for my tenth birthday, and I almost broke my leg trying to ride it. After that, I put it away and refused to touch it again.

"Don't get on that thing!" I yelled at "Gary". "It's dangerous. You might hurt my body. And I want it back in one piece!"

Of course "Gary" didn't even notice me. Instead, he carried the skateboard out in front of the house and put it down on the ground.

A short while later, Kaitlyn and Judy walked up the road. I waited for them to start giggling and making fun of the new me.

"Hi, Gary," Kaitlyn said. She brushed some curly hair off her forehead and smiled. "Are we late for our skateboarding lesson?"

"Gary" flashed her a big smile. "No way, Kaitlyn," he answered in my voice. "Want to head over to the playground like we did yesterday?"

I couldn't believe my ears. Skateboarding lesson? Head over to the playground *like we did yesterday*? What was going on around here?

"I hope you don't mind, Gary," Judy said. "We told some of the other kids—like Gail and Louie—how good you are. They all said they can't wait to take a lesson from you, too. Is that okay? Because if it isn't, we can call them, and—"

"No problem, Jude," "Gary" broke in. "Let's get going, okay?" The new "me" hopped on to his skateboard and smoothly rolled his way down the pavement. Judy and Kaitlyn hurried after him.

For a second, I was too shocked to move. But then I decided to follow them.

As I swooped after them, I kept muttering to myself, "I can't believe it! Lutz the Klutz is giving skateboard lessons at the playground? Everybody's waiting for him to show up? What is going on?"

A few minutes later, the four of us had reached the playground. Sure enough, a whole gang of kids was waiting there for "Gary". He put down his skateboard and started giving everybody pointers on "boarding" as he called it.

I buzzed over to him and started shouting in

his ear again. "Dirk!" I shouted. "Dirk Davis! It's me. The real Gary Lutz!"

Very casually, he swatted me away.

I tried to speak to him again. This time he swatted me really hard, sending me spinning to the ground.

Trying to shake off the pain, I gave up. Dirk isn't going to help me, I realized.

Miss Karmen is my only hope. After all, she was the one with all the equipment. She was the only person who could reverse what she had done.

I flew on to a tree and tried to work out which way to fly. When you're an insect, everything looks different to you. Things that seem small to a person appear huge to a bee. So I wanted to be sure I didn't get myself mixed up and fly off in the wrong direction.

Standing on a big leaf, I gazed up and down the road until I was sure I knew which way to go. As I got ready to take off, a large shadow suddenly loomed over my head. At first, I thought it was a small bird. But then I realized it was a dragonfly.

"Stay calm," I told myself. "A dragonfly is an insect, isn't it? And insects don't eat each other, right?"

I suppose no one had told the dragonfly.

Before I could move, it zoomed down, wrapped its teeth around my middle, and bit me in two.

I uttered a last gasp and waited for everything to go dark.

It took me a few seconds to realize that the dragonfly had turned and buzzed off in the other direction.

My imagination was running away with me. That's what always happened when I got overtired.

I took a deep breath, grateful to still be in one piece. I decided I had to use my remaining strength to get to Miss Karmen at the Person-to-Person Holidays office.

I rose up into the air, looked both ways for oncoming dragonfly traffic, then fluttered away.

After a long, tiring trip, I floated past a street sign that told me I'd made it to the right place. Roach Street.

I buzzed along the pavement until I came to the Person-to-Person building. Then I sat down on the steps and tried to work out how I was going to get inside.

Luckily, as I rested on the warm cement, I saw a postman marching up the street, stopping at each house along his route. Quickly, I flew over to the Person-to-Person entrance and checked it out. Just as I'd hoped, there was a letterbox in the middle of the door.

I buzzed over to the doorknob, and waited for my chance. Slowly, the postman trudged up to the building.

"Hurry up!" I screamed at him. "Do you think I have all day?" Of course he couldn't hear me.

He fumbled around in his bag and pulled out a bundle of letters. Then, slowly, he reached out and pushed open the letterbox.

Before the postman had a chance to react, I swooped down in front of his nose and buzzed right through the letterbox. As I zipped along, I heard him gasp, and I knew he'd seen me. But for once, luck was with me. I moved so quickly, there hadn't been any time for the postman to try to swat me.

My luck held when I flew up the stairs.

I'd just reached the top when the door to Person-to-Person Holidays opened, and a girl about my age came out. She had long, curly red hair and a serious, thoughtful expression on her face. Was she thinking of swapping places with someone?

"Go home!" I shouted at her. "And don't come back. Stay away from this place! Just look what happened to me!"

Even though I was screaming, the girl didn't even turn her head. But she left the door open just long enough for me to buzz into the Person-to-Person office.

I flew across the waiting room and saw Miss Karmen, sitting in the same chair she'd been in when I first met her.

I shot right towards her—and smacked into something hard.

Pain roared through my body. I dropped to the floor, dizzy and confused.

As my head began to clear, I remembered the glass wall separating Miss Karmen from the waiting area. Like some kind of brainless June insect, I'd crashed right into it!

I shook myself to clear my mind. "Miss Karmen!" I yelled. "Miss Karmen. It's me—Gary Lutz. Look what's happened! Can you help me? *Can* you?"

Miss Karmen didn't even glance up from her paperwork. Once again, I realized no one could hear my squeaky insect voice.

With a defeated moan, I sank down on to the seat of the chair and curled up into a tiny ball. I'd come all this way for nothing, I realized. I'd found the one person in the world who might be able to help me. And she couldn't even hear me!

"I give up," I whispered sadly. "It's hopeless. I have to get used to the idea of being a bee for ever! There's no way I'll ever get my old body back."

I had never been so miserable in all my life. I wished someone would come along, drop into the chair, and sit on me!

A strange sound startled me from my unhappy thoughts. I sat up straight and listened hard.

"*Whoo-ah. Whoo-ah.*" It almost sounded like

someone breathing. But how could that be? It was so loud!

I floated up off the chair and buzzed around the room, trying to find out where the sound was coming from. I had circled the room twice before I worked it out.

Miss Karmen was bending over to pick up something she'd dropped on the floor. Her nose and mouth were only centimetres from the top of her desk. And the microphone she used to talk to people had picked up the sounds of her breathing!

Suddenly, I had a brilliant idea. If I could get to the other side of the glass, I could use the microphone to make Miss Karmen hear me.

I swooped over to the wall and flew straight up to the ceiling. No luck there. The sheet of glass went all the way up. There was no space for me to wedge myself through to the other side.

I buzzed down to the place where the glass met the top of Miss Karmen's desk. Yes! There was a small slot in the glass. I remembered how she had passed through the book of photographs on my first visit to the office.

The slot wasn't very large. But it was big enough for my round little bee body.

I shot through the hole and jumped up on top of the microphone.

"Miss Karmen!" I shouted, putting my mouth

next to the hard metal. "Miss Karmen!"

Her eyes opened wide. Her mouth dropped open in confusion. She stared out into the waiting room, searching for the person speaking.

"It's Gary Lutz!" I called out. "And I'm down here on your microphone."

Miss Karmen stared down at the microphone. Then her eyes narrowed in fear. "What's going on? Who's doing this? Is this a joke?"

"No!" I cried. "It's no joke at all. It's really me—Gary Lutz!"

"But—but—" she stammered, but no other words came out. "What's the joke? How are you doing that?"

Her voice was so loud, the sound waves nearly blasted me off the microphone.

"You don't have to yell!" I cried. "I can hear you."

"I don't *believe* this!" she exclaimed in a trembling voice. She stared down at me.

"It's all your fault!" I shouted angrily. "You messed up the transfer operation. When you made the switch, one of my neighbour's bees must have got into the machine. So, instead of putting me into Dirk Davis's body, you put me into a bee!"

Miss Karmen blinked. Then she slapped her forehead. "Well, that explains it!" she cried.

"That explains why Dirk Davis's body has been behaving so strangely."

She picked up some papers on her desk and started putting them into her briefcase. "I really must apologize," she said. "I feel really bad, Gary. We've never had a mix-up like this before. I hope ... I hope it's at least been *interesting* for you."

"Interesting?" I shrieked. "It's been a nightmare! You wouldn't believe what I've been through. I've been attacked by screen doors, cats, flyswatters—you name it! You yourself almost ran me over with your car!"

All the colour drained from her face. "Oh, no," she cried, her voice a whisper. "I'm so sorry. I—I didn't know."

"Well, what about it?" I asked her impatiently.

"What about *what*?"

"What about getting me back into my body! Can you do it right away?"

Miss Karmen cleared her throat. "Well, I *could*," she replied slowly. "Normally, I could transfer you right back. But there's a slight problem in your case."

"What kind of problem?" I demanded.

"It's Dirk Davis," Miss Karmen replied. "It seems he's become very attached to your old body. He likes your house and your parents, too. In fact, he even likes your sister, Krissy!"

"So?" I cried. "So what's that supposed to mean?"

Miss Karmen stood up and pushed in her desk chair. "It *means*," she said, "that Dirk Davis is refusing to give up your old body. He says he absolutely won't go back to his old life. He plans to keep your body for ever."

"*WHAT?*" I screamed, hopping up and down angrily on the microphone.

"Just what I said," Miss Karmen said. "Dirk Davis wants to keep your body for the rest of his life."

"But he can't do that, can he?"

"It is very upsetting," she replied, biting her lower lip. "It wasn't what he said in our original agreement. But if he refuses to get out of your body and your life, there's really nothing I can do."

Miss Karmen gazed down at me sympathetically. "I'm so sorry about this, Gary," she said softly. "I suppose I'll have to be more careful in future."

"What about *my* future? What am I supposed to do now?" I wailed.

Miss Karmen shrugged. "I don't know. Maybe you could go back, wait in the hive—and maybe Dirk Davis will change his mind."

"Back to the hive?!" My antennae stood straight on end, quivering with rage. "Do you have any idea what it's like in there? Cramped together with those hairy bees in the darkness? Listening to that deafening buzz day and night?"

"It's a way of staying alive," Miss Karmen replied bluntly.

"I—I don't care!" I stammered. "I'm never going back there! Never!"

"This is tragic. Tragic!" Miss Karmen cried. "I'll give your case some thought tonight, Gary. I promise. Maybe I can come up with a way of getting your body away from Dirk."

She crossed the room and opened the office door. "I'm so upset. So upset," she murmured. Then she disappeared out of the door, slamming it behind her.

Trembling with anger at Dirk Davis, I hopped down to the desk. "Hey, wait!" I called after her. "You've locked me in!"

Miss Karmen was so upset she forgot about me!

I rose up into the air and started to chase after her. But then, I happened to glance back down at her desk. Dirk Davis's questionnaire was right on top of a pile of papers. His address was next to his name. He lived at 203 Eastwood Avenue.

Eastwood Avenue was near the computer

shop, so I knew where it was. "Maybe the *old* Dirk Davis will know how to get my body back!" I told myself.

It was worth a try. I ducked through the slot in the glass and flew around the waiting room.

No exit. No open window. No crack in the door.

Once again, I was trapped.

Frantically, I buzzed all around the waiting room. Then I went back through the slot in the glass. I checked the whole equipment room. Every window was closed tight.

I flew past a calendar and happened to see the date. "Oh, no!" I cried. "It's Friday! It's the weekend. Miss Karmen might not come back to work for two whole days."

In two days, I realized, I would starve to death!

I *had* to get out! I went over to the far wall and noticed another door I hadn't seen before. I zipped through it.

The room turned out to be a tiny bathroom. With one small window. Which was open just a crack. It was all I needed.

"Hurray!" I yelled. I shot out through the window and sailed into the open air. Then I turned right and headed for Eastwood Avenue. Luckily, it wasn't very far away. All this flying around was really beginning to wear me out.

I found Dirk Davis's house without any trouble. When I got there, I saw "Dirk" himself—or whoever he was now—standing in the front garden. I recognized him from the picture I'd seen in the Person-to-Person album.

"Hey!" I yelled to him. "Hey, er . . . Dirk!"

The tall, good-looking boy turned around and stared at me. His mouth moved, and it looked as if he was saying something.

But I couldn't understand any words. All I heard was a humming sound.

"I'm Gary Lutz!" I cried in my little voice. "Can you help me get Dirk Davis out of my body?"

The boy stared at me. Then he grinned.

I was confused. What was he grinning about?

"Hey, can you hear me?" I cried.

Now "Dirk" motioned with his hand.

"You want me to follow you?" I asked. I felt excited. "Are you taking me somewhere we can get help?"

"Dirk" grinned again. Then he turned and walked round the corner of the house. I didn't know where we were going. But I knew I had to follow him.

I found "Dirk" in the back garden. "Hum," he said to me. "Hum." He pointed to a big rose-bush and grinned. Then he stuck his nose deep inside one of the blossoms. "Hummmmmmmmmm," he said. "Yummmmmmmmm."

I gaped at him in shock. "Of course!" I cried. "You got the bee's mind when I got the bee's body!"

"Dirk" didn't say anything. But when he pulled his face out of the rose, the end of his nose was covered with yellow pollen.

"Dirk" looked a little surprised. And disappointed. I suppose he missed his long, sucking tongue—the tongue that was now hanging off the front of *my* face.

"You can't help me," I muttered to him. "You're in worse shape than I am!"

"Hum?" he replied. "Hum?"

He looked rather silly with that yellow nose. But I felt sorry for him. He and I had the wrong brains in the wrong bodies. I knew exactly how he felt.

"I'm going to go and get help for both of us," I told him. "If I get my body back, maybe you'll get yours, too."

With a loud buzz, I flew out of the Davises' garden. As I left, I thought I heard "Dirk" buzz back at me. I glanced over my wing and saw him sticking his face into another rose. Maybe this time he'd have better luck getting the pollen out.

I headed towards my own house. This time I planned to *make* Dirk Davis give me my body back. Or else.

As I turned up my street, I suddenly heard a

familiar voice coming from behind a tree.

"Don't mess with me! Don't mess with me, man!"

I couldn't believe it. The voice belonged to Marv. But who was he talking to?

I shot around the tree to find out. To my surprise, I saw that Marv was talking to *me*—or, Dirk Davis, in my body. Barry and Karl were right beside me.

Look out, Dirk! I thought. Run! Run!

Please don't let them wreck my body!

But it was too late.

Barry, Marv, and Karl were closing in on him, about to give him the pounding of his life.

I flew closer.

"Look out, Dirk! Look out!" I squeaked.

But to my surprise, the three hulking creeps weren't moving in on "Gary"—they were *backing away* from him!

"Don't mess with me!" Marv cried. "I *said* I was sorry."

"We apologized," Barry whinned. "Don't hit us again, Gary! Please!"

Karl whimpered behind him, nursing a bloody nose.

"You guys are losers," I heard "Gary" tell them. "Take a hike. Go and get a life."

"Okay! Okay!" Marv cried. "Just no more rough stuff, okay, Gary?"

"Gary" shook his head and walked away.

I don't *believe* this! I thought gleefully. Barry, Marv, and Karl were afraid of *me*!

I decided I'd have some fun with them, too.

I swooped down and landed on Barry's nose,

101

buzzing as loudly and menacingly as I could.

"Yowwwww!" he shrieked in surprise—and swatted himself on the nose.

I was too fast for him. I was already on Karl's ear.

Karl cried out and toppled backwards into a thorny rose-bush.

Then I buzzed round and round Marv.

"Get away!" he shouted angrily.

And I flew right into his mouth.

His scream nearly defeated me. But it was worth it.

Marv started spitting and choking and gagging.

I flew up into the air, laughing so hard, I nearly broke my antennae. That was the most fun I'd had since becoming a bee!

I watched the three gorillas run away. Then I flew up the road to my house.

"Gary" had left the window open, and I was able to shoot in. He was lying on my bed, reading one of my comic books and eating crackers with honey on them.

The honey smelled really good, and I realized I was hungry again. I reminded myself to stop by a flower and get a snack the next time I went outside.

But, meanwhile, I had work to do. I flew over and landed on Gary's earlobe.

"Hey, you! Dirk Davis!" I yelled at the top of my little voice. "I need to talk to you!"

He reached a hand up and flicked me off his face. I fell down and landed with a bounce on the bed.

I buzzed angrily and shot right back up his earlobe. "Hey, you! I want my body back! You have to get out of it. Now!"

"Gary" folded up his comic book and swung it at me. I buzzed with rage and frustration. I wasn't going to give up this time. No way! I had to make him hear me.

I rocketed up in the air and landed on the top of his head. Then I climbed down to his other earlobe and tried one more time. "I'm not leaving you alone till you get out of my body!" I screeched. "Do you hear me?"

He sighed and shrugged his shoulders. "Will you *please* stop bothering me?" he asked. "Can't you see I'm trying to relax?"

"You can *hear* me?"

"Yeah. Of course," he muttered. "I can hear you okay."

"You can?" I was so surprised, I almost fell off his ear.

"Yes, I can hear you perfectly. Weird, huh? I'm not sure why. But I think some bee cells got mixed up with my human cells during our electronic transfer. I can hear all kinds of little insect noises now."

"*Your* human cells? Those are *my* human cells!" I cried.

Dirk shrugged.

"Enough chitchat," I told him. "When do you plan to get out of my body?"

"Never," he replied. He picked up his comic book and started reading it again. "I like your body. I can't understand why you gave it up to become a bee."

"That wasn't my idea!" I screamed.

"You've got a good life here," he continued. "I mean, you have great parents. Krissy is an okay sister. And Claus is an awesome cat. It's a shame you didn't know all that when you were in your body. Which is now *my* body!"

"It's not your body! It's mine! Give it back!" I started to buzz furiously all around his head, swooping down in front of his nose, crashing into his ears, batting my wings in his eyes.

Dirk Davis didn't even flinch.

"What's the matter with you, anyway?" I yelled. "You're *me* now. You're supposed to be scared of bees!"

"Gary" laughed. "You've forgotten something," he said. "I'm *not* you. I'm just inside your body. I'm still me inside. And I'm not in the least bit afraid of bees!"

"And now," he went on, "take a hike, okay? Buzz off. I'm busy."

Frozen with anger and disappointment, I

slumped on the bedspread without moving. "Gary" raised the comic book up into the air. "I'd hate to swat you," he said. "But I will if I have to!"

I dodged away just as the comic book slapped down on the bedspread. Then I shot back out of the window.

For a few minutes, I flew aimlessly around, lost in my sad thoughts. Finally, I remembered how hungry I was. I perched on top of a big, orange lily blossom and started sucking up some nectar.

Not bad, I told myself as I drank. But honey on crackers would be much better.

"What am I supposed to do now?" I asked myself. "Am I really doomed to be a bee for the rest of my life?" I pulled my head out of the orange blossom and looked around. "And how long *is* the rest of my life anyway?"

I remembered a page from *The Big Book of Bees*.

"The life of the average bee is not very long. While the queen can live through as many as five winters, the workers and drones die off in the autumn."

In the autumn?

It was already nearly August!

If I stayed in this bee body, I had only a month or two at most!

I gazed sadly up at my house. "Gary" had

turned the light on in my room, and it twinkled in the early evening dusk.

How I wished I could be up there! Why, why had I ever been stupid enough to think I'd be better off in someone else's body?

Then I heard a buzz. I peered over the blossom. Sure enough, I saw a bee.

He hopped up on to the flowers. Two other bees quickly joined him. Then three more. They buzzed angrily.

"Go away!" I cried.

I tried to fly away.

But before I could lift off, they all swarmed over me.

I couldn't move. The bees had taken me prisoner.

"Don't take me back to the hive!" I shrieked. "Don't take me back!"

But to my horror, they started to drag me away.

I struggled to squirm away. But they turned their stingers on me.

Were they some kind of bee police? Did they think I was trying to avoid the hive?

I didn't have a chance to discuss it with them. They lifted me up into the air. There were bees in front of me, bees behind, and bees on all sides.

We flew past my bedroom window. "Help!" I called.

"Gary" glanced up from his plate of crackers and honey. He smiled and waved at me.

I was so angry, I thought I might explode.

But then an idea came to me. A crazy idea. A desperate idea.

I buzzed as loudly as I could. Then I darted out of line and shot into the open bedroom window.

Were the others following me? Were they?

Yes!

They didn't want to let me escape.

"Gary" sat up when he saw me and my buzzing followers. He rolled up his comic book, preparing to swat us.

I circled the room, and the other bees followed.

"Get out! Get out!" "Gary" screamed.

There weren't enough of us, I decided. I needed a huge swarm.

I flew back out of the window. The others buzzed after me.

Now I was the head bee. As fast as I could, I led my group back to Mr Andretti's garage, and in through the hole in the screen.

I hesitated at the hive entrance. I took a deep breath.

Was I really going to go back inside?

I knew I had no choice. "Go for it, Lutz!" I shouted to myself.

I shot in through the entrance hole.

Then I began flying crazily through the hive, buzzing angrily, bumping into the walls, bumping into other bees.

The hive stirred to life.

The buzzing grew to a dull roar. Then a loud roar. Then a *deafening* roar!

Round and round I raged, flying faster and faster, throwing myself frantically against the sticky hive walls, tumbling, darting, buzzing furiously.

The entire hive was in an uproar now.

I had turned the bees into an angry swarm.

108

Out of the hive I flew. Out into the darkening evening. Out through the hole in the screen, up, up, and away.

And the bees swarmed after me, like a black cloud against the grey-blue sky.

Up we soared. Up, up.

A buzzing, swarming cloud.

Up, up.

I led them up to the bedroom window.

Tumbling over each other, raging through the air, we swarmed into "Gary's" room.

"Huh?" He jumped off the bed.

He didn't have time to say a word.

I landed in his hair. The raging swarm followed, buzzing angrily, surrounding him, covering his head, his face, his shoulders.

"H-help!" His weak cry was drowned out by the roar of the bees. "Help me!"

I dropped down on to the tip of Gary's nose. "Have you had enough?" I demanded. "Are you ready to give me back my body?"

"Never!" he cried. "I don't care what you do to me! You'll never get your body back! It's mine, and I'm keeping it for ever!"

Whoooa! I could not believe my ears.

I mean, he was *covered* in bees! And still he wouldn't listen to reason!

I didn't know *what* to do.

The other bees were starting to lose interest. Some of them drifted to the plate of honey. Most of them floated back out of the open window.

"You can't get away with this, Dirk!" I screamed.

With a furious wail, I whirled around. Then I stabbed my razor-sharp stinger deep into the side of "Gary's" nose.

"Owwwwwww!" He let out a high-pitched shriek and grabbed at his nose.

Then he staggered backwards and fell over on to the bed.

"Yaaaaay!" I cried out in celebration.

For one instant, I felt triumphant.

A tiny bee had defeated a huge enemy! I was victorious! I had won a fight against a giant!

My celebration didn't last very long.

I suddenly realized what I had done. And I remembered what happens to a bee after it stings someone.

"I'm going to die," I murmured weakly. "I've stung someone, and now I'm going to die!"

Weaker.

I felt the strength drain from me.

Weaker and weaker.

"What have I done?" I asked myself. "I gave up my life for the chance to sting Dirk Davis! Why was I such a fool?"

I struggled to keep my wings moving, struggled to stay in the air.

I knew I was doomed. But I wanted to stay alive as long as I could. Maybe, I thought, as I felt my strength fading, maybe I'll have a chance to say goodbye to my family.

"Mum! Dad! Krissy!" I buzzed faintly. "Where are you?"

It was hard to breathe. I felt so tired, so weak.

I floated out of the window and sank to the grass below.

I thought I recognized the shape of the old maple tree where I used to read books and spy on Mr Andretti. But my sight was so bad, it was hard to be sure about anything. The whole world swirled in grey shadows.

I could no longer hold up my head. The grey shadows grew darker and darker.

Until the world faded completely from view.

I sat up slowly. The ground spun beneath me.

Where was I?

My back garden?

I blinked, struggling to bring it all into focus, waiting for my eyes to clear.

"There's the old maple tree!" I cried. "And there's my house! And there's Mr Andretti's house!"

Was I alive?

Was I really alive, sitting in my back garden seeing all the familiar places?

Did I have my strength back?

I decided to test it. I tried to spread my wings and fly up into the air.

But for some reason, my wings didn't seem to be working. My body felt heavy and strange.

I frowned and looked down, inspecting myself to see what was wrong. "Whoooa!" I cried out in surprise. Instead of six legs, I saw two arms and two legs and my skinny old body.

Breathlessly, I reached up to touch my face. My extra eyes were gone—and so were my antennae, and my layer of feathery fuzz. Instead, I felt hair! And smooth, human skin!

I jumped up and shouted for joy. "I'm a person again! I'm me! I'm me!"

I threw my arms around my chest and gave myself a hug. Then I danced around the back garden, testing my arms and legs.

They worked! They all worked!

I couldn't get over how wonderful it was to be human again!

"But how did it happen?" I asked myself. "What happened to Dirk Davis?"

For a chilling instant, I wondered if Dirk had been forced into a bee's body the way I had.

Probably not, I decided.

But what had happened?

How did I get my body back?

Was it the bee sting? Did the shock of the sting send us all back to the bodies we belonged in?

"I've got to call Miss Karmen and find out!" I realized.

But for now, all I wanted to do was see my family.

I hurried up the back steps and into the house. As I ran through the kitchen, I crashed right into Krissy. As usual, she was carrying Claus under one arm.

"Watch where you're going!" Krissy snapped at me.

She probably expected me to snap back at her and try to push her out of my way. But instead I

113

grabbed her shoulders and gave her a big hug. Then I planted a kiss on her cheek.

"Yuck! Disgusting!" she cried and wiped the cheek with her hand.

I laughed happily.

"Don't give me your fleas, creep!" Krissy cried.

"You're a creep!" I replied.

"No, *you're* a creep!" she repeated.

"You're a pig!" I shouted.

It felt so good to be calling her names again!

I gleefully called her a few more things. Then I hurried upstairs to see my parents.

I met them as they were coming out of my room.

"Mum! Dad!" I cried. I hurried to them, planning to throw my arms around them.

But they thought I was just trying to get into my room. "Don't go in there, Gary," warned my dad. "You left your window open again, and a swarm of bees got in there."

"You'd better go next door," Mum said. "Get Mr Andretti. He'll know how to get them out."

I couldn't hold back any longer. I threw my arms around my mother's neck and gave her a big kiss. "Mum, I've missed you so much!"

My mother hugged me back, but I saw her exchange a curious look with my dad. "Gary?" she asked. "Are you okay? How could you miss me when you've been right here in this house?"

"Well . . ." I thought fast. "I meant that I missed spending time with you. We really need to do more things together."

My mother spread one hand over my forehead. "No. No temperature," she told my father.

"Gary," Dad said impatiently. "Would you mind running over and getting Mr Andretti? If we don't get those bees out of your room, you'll never be able to go to sleep tonight!"

"Bees?" I said casually. "Hey, no problem. I'll take care of them."

I reached out and started to open my door. Before I could, Dad grabbed my arm. "Gary!" he cried in alarm. "What's the matter with you? There are bees in your room! B-E-E-S. Don't you remember—you're scared of bees!"

I stared back at him and thought about what he'd said. To my surprise, I realized I was no longer the slightest bit scared of bees! In fact, I was actually looking forward to seeing them again.

"No problem, Dad," I told him. "I think I must have outgrown that, or something."

I opened the door and went into my room. Sure enough, there was the old swarm, buzzing away over the plate of honey and crackers on the bed.

"Hi, guys!" I said cheerfully. "Time to leave now!"

I walked over to the bed and waved my hands at them, trying to shoo them back out of the window. A few of them buzzed angrily at me.

I laughed to myself. Then I picked up the plate of crackers and honey and chucked it out of the window. "Go and get it!" I told them.

I shooed them gently out of the window.

"Goodbye!" I called to them as they left. "Thanks! Take good care of the honeycombs! I'll try to visit as soon as I can!"

When the last bee was gone, I turned around and saw my parents. They were standing absolutely motionless in the doorway, staring at me, frozen with shock.

"Dad?" I said. "Mum?"

My dad blinked and seemed to come back to life. He crossed the room and put a hand on my shoulder. "Gary? Are you feeling all right?"

"Just fine," I replied, grinning happily. "Just fine."

That whole crazy adventure happened about a month ago.

Now it's nearly autumn. I'm still sitting in my favourite place under the maple tree in the back garden, reading a book and chomping down tortilla chips.

I just love coming out here. All the autumn-flowering plants are in bloom, and the garden is really pretty.

I've been spending the last few days of my summer holiday relaxing back here. Of course, I also go to the playground a lot.

The other day I ran into that girl with the red hair I saw coming out of the Person-to-Person office. We started talking, and I didn't trip over my own feet or anything. She seems very nice. I hope she doesn't plan to swap lives with any-body else!

That conversation and a lot of things have

made me realize that my short life as a bee really changed me.

First of all, it taught me to appreciate my family for the first time ever. My parents are pretty nice. And my sister is okay. For a sister.

And now, I'm not scared of any of the things I used to be scared of. Yesterday, I walked right past Marv, Barry, and Karl, and I didn't bat an eyelid.

In fact, when I remembered how I buzzed at them, I almost burst out laughing.

I'm not at all scared of them any more. And I'm different in other ways, too.

I'm a lot better at sports and bike riding and things. And I'm a great skateboarder now. In fact, I still give lessons. Judy and Kaitlyn hang around me all the time. And Gail and Louie, too.

The other day, I actually ran into Dirk Davis at the playground. At first, I didn't want to talk to him. But then he turned out to be pretty nice.

He apologized to me. "I'm sorry I tried to steal your body," he said. "But things didn't turn out so well for me, either. That bee failed all my maths tests in summer school!"

We both had a good laugh about that. And now Dirk and I are friends.

So all in all, my life is back to normal.

I feel terrific, totally normal.

In fact, I feel much better than normal.

It's so great to sit here in the back garden,

reading and relaxing, smelling the fresh autumn air, enjoying the flowers.

Mmmmmm.

Those hollyhocks are really beautiful.

Excuse me a moment while I get up and take a closer look.

That blossom down near the ground is so perfect.

I think I'll get down on my knees to take a quick taste.

Do you know how to suck the pollen out?

I've worked out the best way. It's not as hard as it looks.

You just purse your lips and stick your tongue out like this, see?

Then you dip your face down into the blossom and suck up all the pollen you want.

Try it.

Go ahead.

Mmmmmmmm.

Go ahead. It's easy. Really!

Deep Trouble

There I was, two hundred feet under the sea.

I was on the hunt of my life. The hunt for the Great White Stingray.

That's what they called him at Coast Guard Headquarters. But, me, I called him Joe.

The giant stingray had already stung ten swimmers. People were afraid to step into the water. Panic spread all up and down the coast.

That's why they sent for me.

William Deep, Jr., of Baltimore, Maryland.

Yes, William Deep, Jr., world-famous twelve-year-old undersea explorer. Solver of scary ocean problems.

I captured the Great White Shark that terrorized Myrtle Beach. I proved he wasn't so great!

I fought the giant octopus that ate the entire California Championship Surfing Team.

I unplugged the electric eel that sent shock waves all over Miami.

But now I faced the fight of my life. Joe, the Great White Stingray.

Somewhere down deep under the sea, he lurked.

I had everything I needed: scuba suit, flippers, mask, oxygen tank, and poison-dart gun.

Wait—did something move? Just behind that giant clam?

I raised my dart gun and waited for an attack.

Then, suddenly, my mask clouded. I couldn't breathe.

I strained for breath. No air came.

My oxygen tank! Someone must have tampered with it!

There was no time to lose. Two hundred feet down—and no air! I had to surface—fast!

I kicked my legs, desperately trying to pull myself to the surface.

Holding my breath. My lungs about to burst. I was losing strength, getting dizzy.

Would I make it? Or would I die right here, deep under the ocean, Joe the Stingray's dinner?

Panic swept over me like an ocean tide. I searched through the fogged mask for my diving partner. Where was she when I needed her?

Finally, I spotted her swimming up at the surface, near the boat.

Help me! Save me! No air! I tried to tell her, waving my arms like a maniac.

Finally she noticed me. She swam towards me

and dragged my dazed and limp body to the surface.

I ripped off my mask and sucked in mouthfuls of air.

"What's your problem, Aqua Man?" she cried. "Did a jellyfish sting you?"

My diving partner is very brave. She laughs in the face of danger.

I struggled to catch my breath. "No air. Someone—cut off—tank—"

Then everything went black.

125

My diving partner shoved my head back under the water. I opened my eyes and came up sputtering.

"Get real, Billy," she said. "Can't you snorkel without acting like a total jerk?"

I sighed. She was no fun.

My "diving partner" was really just my bratty sister, Sheena. I was only pretending to be William Deep, Jr., undersea explorer.

But would it kill Sheena to go along with it just once?

My name actually *is* William Deep, Jr., but everybody calls me Billy. I'm twelve—I think I mentioned that already.

Sheena is ten. She looks like me. We both have straight black hair, but mine is short and hers goes down to her shoulders. We're both skinny, with knobbly knees and elbows, and long, narrow feet. We both have dark blue eyes and thick, dark eyebrows.

Other than that, we're not alike at all.

Sheena has no imagination. She was never afraid of monsters in her cupboard when she was little. She didn't believe in Santa Claus or the tooth fairy, either. She loves to say, "There's no such thing."

I dived underwater and pinched Sheena's leg. *Attack of the Giant Lobster Man!*

"Stop it!" she screamed. She kicked me in the shoulder. I came up for air.

"Hey, you two," my uncle said. "Be careful down there."

My uncle stood on the desk of his sea lab boat, the *Cassandra*. He peered down at Sheena and me snorkelling nearby.

My uncle's name is George Deep, but everybody calls him Dr D. Even my dad, who is his brother, calls him Dr D. Maybe that's because he looks just the way a scientist should.

Dr D is short, thin, wears glasses and a very serious, thoughtful expression. He has curly brown hair and a bald spot at the back of his head. Anyone who saw him would say, "I bet you're a scientist."

Sheena and I were visiting Dr D on the *Cassandra*. Every year our parents let us spend our summer vacation with Dr D. It sure beats hanging out at home. This summer, we were anchored just off a tiny island called Ilandra, in the Caribbean Sea.

Dr D is a marine biologist. He specializes in tropical marine life. He studies the habits of tropical fish and looks for new kinds of ocean plants and fish that haven't been discovered yet.

The *Cassandra* is a big and sturdy boat. It is about fifty feet long. Dr D uses most of the space for labs and research rooms. Up on deck is a cockpit, where he steers the boat. He keeps a dinghy tied to the starboard, or right side of the deck, and a huge glass tank on the port, or left side.

Sometimes Dr D catches very big fish and keeps them temporarily in the glass tank—usually just long enough to tag the fish for research, or care for them if they are sick or injured.

The rest of the deck is open space, good for playing catch or sunbathing.

Dr D's research takes him all over the world. He isn't married and doesn't have any kids. He says he's too busy staring at fish.

But he likes kids. That's why he invites me and Sheena to visit him every summer.

"Stick close together, kids," Dr D said. "And don't swim off too far. Especially you, Billy."

He narrowed his eyes at me. That's his "I mean it" look. He never narrows his eyes at Sheena.

"There've been reports of some shark sightings in the area," he said.

128

"Sharks! Wow!" I said.

Dr D frowned at me. "Billy," he said. "This is serious. Don't leave the boat. And don't go near the reef."

I knew he was going to say that.

Clamshell Reef is a long, red coral reef just a few hundred yards away from where we were anchored. I'd been dying to explore it ever since we got there.

"Don't worry about me, Dr D," I called up to him. "I won't get into trouble."

Sheena muttered under her breath, "Yeah, right."

I reached out to give her another lobster pinch, but she dived under the water.

"Good," said Dr D. "Now don't forget—if you see a shark fin, try not to splash around a lot. Movement will attract it. Just slowly, steadily return to the boat."

"We won't forget," said Sheena, who had come up behind me, splashing like crazy.

I couldn't help feeling just a little bit excited. I'd always wanted to see a real, live shark.

I'd seen sharks at the aquarium, of course. But they were trapped in a glass tank, where they just swam around restlessly, perfectly harmless.

Not very exciting.

I wanted to spot a shark's fin on the horizon, floating over the water, closer, closer, heading right for us . . .

129

In other words, I wanted adventure.

The *Cassandra* was anchored out in the ocean, a few hundred yards away from Clamshell Reef. The reef surrounded the island. Between the reef and the island stretched a beautiful lagoon.

Nothing was going to stop me from exploring that lagoon—no matter what Dr D said.

"Come on, Billy," Sheena called, adjusting her mask. "Let's check out that school of fish."

She pointed to a patch of tiny ripples in the water near the bow of the boat. She slid the mouthpiece into her mouth and lowered her head into the water. I followed her to the ripples.

Soon Sheena and I were surrounded by hundreds of tiny, neon-blue fish.

Underwater, I always felt as if I were in a faraway world. Breathing through the snorkel, I could live down here with the fish and the dolphins, I thought. After a while, maybe I would grow flippers and a fin.

The tiny blue fish began to swim away, and I swam with them. They were so great-looking! I didn't want them to leave me behind.

Suddenly, the fish all darted from view. I tried to follow, but they were too fast.

They had vanished!

Had something scared them away?

I glanced around. Clumps of seaweed floated near the surface. Then I saw a flash of red.

I floated closer, peering through the mask. A

few yards ahead of me I saw bumpy red formations. Red coral.

Oh, no, I thought. Clamshell Reef. Dr D told me not to swim this far.

I began to turn round. I knew I should swim back to the boat.

But I was tempted to stay and explore a little. After all, I was already there.

The reef looked like a red sandcastle, filled with underwater caves and tunnels. Small fish darted in and out of them. The fish were bright yellow and blue.

Maybe I could swim over and explore one of those tunnels, I thought. How dangerous could it be?

Suddenly, I felt something brush against my leg. It tickled and sent a tingle up my leg.

A fish?

I glanced around, but I didn't see anything.

Then I felt it again.

A tingling against my leg.

And then it clutched me.

Again I turned to see what it was. Again I saw nothing.

My heart began to race. I knew it was probably nothing dangerous. But I wished I could see it.

I turned and started back for the boat, kicking hard.

But something grabbed my right leg—and held on!

I froze in fear. Then I frantically kicked my leg as hard as I could.

Let go! Let go of me!

I couldn't see it—and I couldn't pull free!

The water churned and tossed as I kicked with all my strength.

Overcome with terror, I lifted my head out of the water and choked out a weak cry: "Help!"

But it was no use.

Whatever it was, it kept pulling me down. Down.

Down to the bottom of the sea.

"Help!" I cried out again. "Sheena! Dr D!"

I was dragged below the surface again. I felt the slimy tentacle tighten around my ankle.

As I sank underwater, I turned—and saw it.

It loomed huge and dark.

A sea monster!

Through the churning waters, it glared at me with one giant brown eye. The terrifying creature floated underwater like an enormous, dark green balloon. Its mouth opened in a silent cry, revealing two rows of jagged, sharp teeth.

An enormous octopus! But it had at least *twelve* tentacles!

Twelve long, slimy tentacles. One was wrapped around my ankle. Another one slid towards me.

NO!

My arms thrashed the water.

I gulped in mouthfuls of air.

I struggled to the surface—but the huge creature dragged me down again.

I couldn't believe it. As I sank, scenes from my life actually flashed before my eyes.

I saw my parents, waving to me as I boarded the yellow school bus for my first day of school.

Mum and Dad! I'll never see them again!

What a way to go, I thought. Killed by a sea monster!

No one will believe it.

Everything started to turn red. I felt dizzy, weak.

But something was pulling me, pulling me up.

Up to the surface. Away from the tentacled monster.

I opened my eyes, choking and sputtering.

I stared up at Dr D!

"Billy! Are you all right?" Dr D studied me with concern.

I coughed and nodded. I kicked my right leg. The slimy tentacle was gone.

The dark creature had vanished.

"I heard you screaming and saw you thrashing about," said Dr D. "I swam over from the boat as fast as I could. What happened?"

Dr D had a yellow life-jacket over his shoulders. He slipped a rubber lifebelt over my head. I floated easily now, the lifebelt under my arms.

I had lost my flippers in the struggle. My mask and snorkel dangled around my neck.

Sheena swam over and floated beside me, treading water.

"It grabbed my leg!" I cried breathlessly. "It tried to pull me under!"

"What grabbed your leg, Billy?" asked Dr D. "I don't see anything around here—"

"It was a sea monster," I told him. "A huge one! I felt its slimy tentacle grabbing my leg . . . *Ouch!*"

Something pinched my toe.

"It's back!" I shrieked in horror.

Sheena popped out of the water and shook her wet hair, laughing.

"That was me, you dork!" she cried.

"Billy, Billy," Dr D murmured. "You and your wild imagination." He shook his head. "You nearly scared me to death. Please—don't ever do that again. Your leg probably got tangled in a piece of seaweed, that's all."

"But—but—!" I sputtered.

He dipped his hand in the water and pulled up a handful of slimy green strings. "There's seaweed everywhere."

"But I saw it!" I shouted. "I saw its tentacles, its big, pointy teeth!"

"There's no such thing as sea monsters," said Sheena. Miss Know-It-All.

"Let's discuss it on the boat," my uncle said, dropping the clump of seaweed back in the water. "Come on. Swim back with me. And

135

stay away from the reef. Swim around it."

He turned around and started swimming towards the *Cassandra*. I saw that the sea monster had pulled me into the lagoon. The reef lay between us and the boat. But there was a break in the reef we could swim through.

I followed them, thinking angry thoughts.

Why didn't they believe me?

I had seen the creature grab my leg. It wasn't a stupid clump of seaweed. It wasn't my imagination.

I was determined to prove them wrong. I'd find that creature and show it to them myself— someday. But not today.

Now I was ready to get back to the safety of the boat.

I swam up to Sheena and called, "Race you to the boat."

"Last one there is a chocolate-covered jelly-fish!" she cried.

Sheena can't refuse a race. She started speeding towards the boat, but I caught her by the arm.

"Wait," I said. "Not fair. You're wearing flippers. Take them off."

"Too bad!" she cried, and pulled away. "See you at the boat!" I watched her splash away, building a good lead.

She's not going to win, I decided.

I stared at the reef up ahead.

It would be faster just to swim over the reef. A short cut.

I turned and started to swim straight towards the red coral.

"Billy! Get back here!" Dr D shouted.

I pretended I didn't hear him.

The reef loomed ahead. I was almost there.

I saw Sheena splashing ahead of me. I kicked extra hard. I knew she'd never have the guts to swim over the reef. She'd swim around the end of it. I would cut through and beat her.

But my arms suddenly began to ache. I wasn't used to swimming so far.

Maybe I can stop at the reef and rest my arms for a second, I thought.

I reached the reef. I turned round. Sheena was swimming to the left, around the reef. I could spare a few seconds to rest.

I stepped on to the red coral reef—

—and screamed in horror!

137

My foot burned as if it were on fire. The throbbing pain shot up my leg.

I screamed and dived into the water.

When I surfaced, I heard Sheena yelling, "Dr D! Come quick!"

My foot burned, even in the cold ocean water.

Dr D came up beside me. "Billy, what's the problem now?" he demanded.

"I saw him do something really stupid," Sheena said, smirking.

If my foot hadn't been burning up, I definitely would have punched out her lights.

"My foot!" I moaned. "I stepped on the reef—and—and—"

Dr D held on to the lifebelt around my waist. "Ow. That's painful," he said, reaching up to pat my shoulder. "But you'll be all right. The burning will stop in a little while."

He pointed to the reef. "All that bright red coral is fire coral."

"Huh? Fire coral?" I stared back at it.

"Even I knew that!" Sheena said.

"It's covered with a mild poison," my uncle continued. "When it touches your skin, it burns like fire."

Now he tells me, I thought.

"Don't you know *anything*?" Sheena asked sarcastically.

She was asking for it. She really was.

"You're lucky you only burned your foot," Dr D said. "Coral can be very sharp. You could have cut your foot and got poison into your bloodstream. Then you'd *really* be in trouble."

"Wow! What kind of trouble?" Sheena asked. She seemed awfully eager to hear about all the terrible things that could have happened to me.

Dr D's expression turned serious. "The poison could paralyse you," he said.

"Oh, great," I said.

"So keep away from the red coral from now on," Dr D warned. "And stay away from the lagoon, too."

"But that's where the sea monster lives!" I protested. "We have to go back there. I have to show it to you!"

Sheena bobbed in the blue-green water. "No such thing, no such thing," she chanted. Her favourite phrase. "No such thing—right, Dr D?"

"Well, you never know," Dr D replied thoughtfully. "We don't know all of the creatures that

139

live in the oceans, Sheena. It's better to say that scientists have never seen one."

"So there, She-Ra," I said.

Sheena spit a stream of water at me. She hates it when I call her She-Ra.

"Listen, kids—I'm serious about staying away from this area," said Dr D. "There may not be a sea monster in that lagoon, but there could be sharks, poisonous fish, electric eels. Any number of dangerous creatures. Don't swim over there."

He paused and frowned at me, as if to make sure I'd been paying attention.

"How's your foot feeling, Billy?" he asked.

"It's a little better now," I told him.

"Good. Enough adventure for one morning. Let's get back to the boat. It's almost lunch-time."

We all started swimming back to the *Cassandra*.

As I kicked, I felt something tickle my leg again.

Seaweed?

No.

It brushed against my thigh like—*fingers*.

"Cut it out, Sheena," I shouted angrily. I spun round to splash water in her face.

But she wasn't there. She wasn't anywhere near me.

She was up ahead, swimming beside Dr D.

Sheena couldn't possibly have tickled me.

But something definitely *did*.

I stared down at the water, suddenly gripped with terror.

What was down there?

Why was it teasing me like that?

Was it preparing to grab me again and pull me down for ever?

Alexander DuBrow, Dr D's assistant, helped us aboard the boat.

"Hey, I heard shouting," Alexander said. "Is everything okay?"

"Everything is fine, Alexander," said Dr D. "Billy stepped on some fire coral, but he's all right."

As I climbed up the ladder, Alexander grabbed my hands and pulled me aboard.

"Wow, Billy," he said. "Fire coral. I accidentally bumped into the fire coral my first day here. I saw stars. I really did, man. You sure you're okay?"

I nodded and showed him my foot. "It feels better now. But that wasn't the worst thing that happened. I was almost eaten by a sea monster!"

"No such thing, no such thing," Sheena chanted.

"I really saw it," I insisted. "They don't

believe me. But it was there. In the lagoon. It was big and green and—"

Alexander smiled. "If you say so, Billy," he said. He winked at Sheena.

I wanted to punch out his lights, too.

Big deal science student. What did *he* know?

Alexander was in his early twenties. But, unlike Dr D, he didn't look like a scientist.

He looked more like a football player. He was very tall, about six feet four inches, and muscular. He had thick, wavy, blond hair and blue eyes that crinkled in the corners. He had broad shoulders, and big, powerful-looking hands. He spent a lot of time in the sun and had a smooth, dark tan.

"I hope you're all hungry," Alexander said. "I made chicken salad sandwiches for lunch."

"Oh. Great," Sheena said, rolling her eyes.

Alexander did most of the cooking. He thought he was good at it. But he wasn't.

I went below deck to my cabin to change out of my wet bathing suit. My cabin was really just a tiny sleeping cubby with a cupboard for my things. Sheena had one just like it. Dr D and Alexander had bigger cabins that they could actually walk around in.

We ate in the galley, which was what Dr D called the boat's kitchen. It had a built-in table and built-in seats, and a small area for cooking.

When I entered the galley, Sheena was already

sitting at the table. There was a big sandwich on a plate in front of her, and one waiting for me.

Neither of us was too eager to try Alexander's chicken salad. The night before, we had had brussels sprouts casserole. For breakfast this morning, he had served us wholewheat pancakes that sank to the bottom of my stomach like the *Titanic* going down!

"You first," I whispered to my sister.

"Uh-uh," Sheena said, shaking her head. "You try it. You're older."

My stomach growled. I sighed. There was nothing to do but taste it.

I sank my teeth into the sandwich and started chewing.

Not bad, I thought at first. A little chicken, a little mayonnaise. It actually tasted like a normal chicken salad sandwich.

Then, suddenly, my tongue started to burn. My whole mouth was on fire!

I let out a cry and grabbed for the glass of iced tea in front of me. I downed the entire glass.

"Fire coral!" I screamed. "You put fire coral in the chicken salad!"

Alexander laughed. "Just a little chilli pepper. For taste. You like it?"

"I think I'd rather have cereal for lunch," Sheena said, setting down her sandwich. "If you don't mind."

"You can't have cereal for every meal,"

144

Alexander replied, frowning. "No wonder you're so skinny, Sheena. You never eat anything but cereal. Where's your spirit of adventure?"

"I think I'll have cereal, too," I said sheepishly. "Just for a change of pace."

Dr D came into the galley. "What's for lunch?" he asked.

"Chicken salad sandwiches," said Alexander. "I made them spicy."

"*Very* spicy," I warned him.

Dr D glanced at me and raised an eyebrow. "Oh, really?" he said. "You know, I'm not very hungry. I think I'll just have cereal for lunch."

"Maybe Billy and I could make dinner tonight," Sheena offered. She poured cereal into a bowl and added milk. "It's not fair for Alexander to cook *all* the time."

"That's a nice idea, Sheena," said Dr D. "What do you two know how to make?"

"I know how to make brownies from a mix," I offered.

"And I know how to make fudge," said Sheena.

"Hmm," said Dr D. "Maybe *I'll* cook tonight. How does grilled fish sound?"

"Great!" I said.

After lunch, Dr D went into his office to go over some notes. Alexander led Sheena and me into the main lab to show us around.

The work lab was really cool. It had three big glass tanks along the wall filled with weird, amazing fish.

The smallest tank held two bright yellow sea horses and an underwater trumpet. The underwater trumpet was a long, red-and-white fish shaped like a tube. There were also a lot of guppies swimming around in this tank.

Another tank held some flame angelfish, which were orange-red like fire, and a harlequin tuskfish, with orange-and-aqua tiger stripes for camouflage.

The biggest tank held a long, black-and-yellow, snakelike thing with a mouth full of teeth.

"Ugh!" Sheena made a disgusted face as she stared at the long fish. "That one is really horrid!"

"That's a black ribbon eel," said Alexander. "He bites, but he's not deadly. We call him Biff."

I snarled through the glass at Biff, but he ignored me.

I wondered what it would be like to come face to face with Biff in the ocean. His teeth looked nasty, but he wasn't nearly as big as the sea monster. I figured William Deep, Jr., world-famous undersea explorer, could handle it.

I turned away from the fish tanks and stood by the control panel, staring at all the knobs and dials.

"What does this do?" I asked. I pushed a button. A loud horn blared. We all jumped, startled.

"It honks the horn," Alexander said, laughing.

"Dr D told Billy not to touch things without asking first," said Sheena. "He's told him a million times. He never listens."

"Shut up, She-Ra!" I said sharply.

"*You* shut up."

"Hey—no problem," said Alexander, raising both hands, motioning for us to calm down. "No harm done."

I turned back to the panel. Most of the dials were lit up, with little red indicators moving across their faces. I noticed one dial that was dark, its red indicator still.

"What's this for?" I asked, pointing to the dark dial. "It looks like you forgot to turn it on."

"Oh, that controls the Nansen bottle," Alexander said. "It's broken."

"What's a Nansen bottle?" asked Sheena.

"It collects samples of seawater from way down deep," said Alexander.

"Why don't you mend it?" I asked.

"We can't afford it," said Alexander.

"Why not?" asked Sheena. "Doesn't the university give you money?"

We both knew that Dr D's research was paid for by a university in Ohio.

147

"They gave us money for our research," Alexander explained. "But it's almost gone. We're waiting to see if they'll give us more. In the meantime, we don't have the money to mend things."

"What if the *Cassandra* breaks down or something?" I asked.

"Then I guess we'll have to put her in dry dock for a while," said Alexander. "Or else find a new way to get more money."

"Wow," said Sheena. "That would mean no more summer visits."

I hated to think of the *Cassandra* just sitting in a dock. Even worse was the thought of Dr D being stuck on land with no fish to study.

Our uncle was miserable whenever we had to go ashore. He didn't feel comfortable unless he was on a boat. I know, because one Christmas he came to our house to visit.

Usually Dr D is fun to be with. But that Christmas visit was a nightmare.

Dr D spent the whole time pacing through the house. He barked orders at us like a sea captain.

"Billy, sit up straight!" he yelled at me. "Sheena, swab the decks!"

He just wasn't himself.

Finally, on Christmas Eve, my dad couldn't take it any more. He told Dr D to shape up or ship out.

Dr D ended up spending a good part of

Christmas Day in the bathtub playing with my old toy boats. As long as he stayed in the water, he was back to normal.

I never wanted to see Dr D stranded on land again.

"Don't worry, kids," Alexander said. "Dr D has always found a way to get by."

I hoped Alexander was right.

I studied another strange dial, marked SONAR PROBES.

"Hey, Alexander," I said. "Will you show me how the sonar probes work?"

"Sure," said Alexander. "Just let me finish a few chores."

He walked over to the first fish tank. He scooped out a few guppies with a small net.

"Who wants to feed Biff today?"

"Not me," said Sheena. "Yuck!"

"No way!" I said as I stepped to a porthole and peered out.

I thought I heard a motor outside. So far we had seen very few other boats. Not many people passed by Ilandra.

A white boat chugged up to the side of the *Cassandra*. It was smaller but newer than our boat. A logo on the side said MARINA ZOO.

A man and a woman stood on the deck of the zoo boat. They were both neatly dressed in khaki trousers and button-down shirts. The man had a short, neat haircut, and the woman's brown hair

149

was pulled back in a ponytail. She carried a black briefcase.

The man waved to someone on the deck of the *Cassandra*. I guessed he must be waving at Dr D.

Now Sheena and Alexander stood beside me at the porthole, watching.

"Who's that?" Sheena asked.

Alexander cleared his throat. "I'd better go and see what this is about," he said.

He handed Sheena the net with the guppies in it. "Here," he said. "Feed Biff. I'll be back later."

He left the lab in a hurry.

Sheena looked at the squirming guppies in the net and made a face.

"I'm not going to stay here and watch Biff eat these poor guppies." She stuck the net in my hand and ran out of the cabin.

I didn't want to watch Biff eat the poor fish, either. But I didn't know what else to do with them.

I quickly dumped the guppies into Biff's tank. The eel's head shot forward. His teeth clamped down on a fish. The guppy disappeared. Biff grabbed for another one.

He was a fast eater.

I dropped the net on a table and walked out of the lab.

I made my way down the narrow passageway, planning to go up on deck for some air.

I wondered if Dr D would let me do some more snorkelling this afternoon.

If he said yes, maybe I would swim towards the lagoon, see if I could find any sign of the sea monster.

Was I scared?

Yes.

But I was also determined to prove to my sister and uncle that I wasn't crazy. That I wasn't making it up.

I was passing Dr D's office when I heard voices. I guessed Dr D and Alexander must be in there with the two people from the zoo.

I paused for just a second. I didn't mean to eavesdrop, I swear. But the man from the zoo had a loud voice, and I couldn't help but hear him.

And what he said was the most amazing thing I had ever heard in my whole, entire life.

"I don't care how you do it, Dr Deep," the man bellowed. "But I want you to find that mermaid!"

A mermaid!

Was he serious?

I couldn't believe it. Did he really want my uncle to find a real, live mermaid?

I knew Sheena would start chanting, "No such thing, no such thing." But here was a grown man, a man who worked for a zoo, talking about a mermaid. It *had* to be real!

My heart started to pound with excitement. I might be one of the first people on Earth ever to see a mermaid! I thought.

And then I had an even better thought: *What if I was the one to find her?*

I'd be famous! I'd be on TV and everything!

William Deep, Jr., the famous sea explorer!

Well, after I heard that, I couldn't just walk away. I had to hear more.

Holding my breath, I pressed my ear to the door and listened.

"Mr Showalter, Ms Wickman, please understand," I heard Dr D saying. "I'm a scientist, not a circus trainer. My work is serious. I can't waste any time looking for fairy tale creatures."

"We're quite serious, Dr Deep," said Ms Wickman. "There is a mermaid in these waters. And if anyone can find her, you can."

I heard Alexander ask, "What makes you think there's really a mermaid out there?"

"A fisherman from a nearby island spotted her," replied the man from the zoo. "He said he got pretty close to her—and he's sure she's real. He saw her near the reef—*this* reef, just off Ilandra."

The reef! Maybe she lives in the lagoon!

I leaned closer to the door. I didn't want to miss a word of this.

"Some of these fishermen are very superstitious, Mr Showalter," my uncle scoffed. "For years there have been stories . . . but no real reason to believe them."

"We didn't believe the man ourselves," said the woman. "Not at first. But we asked some other fishermen in the area, and they claim to have seen the mermaid, too. And I think they're telling the truth. Their descriptions of her match, down to the smallest detail."

I could hear my uncle's desk chair creak. I imagined him leaning forward as he asked, "And how, exactly, did they describe her?"

"They said she looked like a young girl," Mr Showalter told him. "Except for the—" he cleared his throat—"the fish tail. She's small, delicate, with long, blonde hair."

"They described her tail as shiny and bright green," said the woman. "I know it sounds incredible, Dr Deep. But when we spoke to the fishermen, we were convinced that they really saw a mermaid!"

There was a pause.

Was I missing something? I pressed my ear to the door. I heard my uncle ask, "And why, exactly, do you want to capture this mermaid?"

"Obviously, a real, live mermaid would be a spectacular attraction at a zoo like ours," said the woman. "People from all over the world would flock to see her. The Marina Zoo would make millions of pounds."

"We are prepared to pay you very well for your trouble, Dr Deep," said Mr Showalter. "I understand you are running out of money. What if the university refuses to give you more? It would be terrible if you had to stop your important work just because of that."

"The Marina Zoo can promise you one million pounds," said the woman. "*If* you find the mermaid. I'm sure your lab could run for a long time on that much money."

A million pounds! I thought. How could Dr D turn down that kind of money?

My heart pounded with excitement. I pushed against the door, straining to hear.

What would my uncle's answer be?

Leaning hard against the door, I heard Dr D let out a long, low whistle. "That's quite a lot of money, Ms Wickman," I heard him say.

There was a long pause. Then he continued. "But even if mermaids existed, I wouldn't feel right about capturing one for a zoo to put on display."

"I promise you we would take excellent care of her," replied Mr Showalter. "Our dolphins and whales are very well cared for. The mermaid, of course, would get extra-special treatment."

"And, remember, Dr Deep," said Ms Wickman. "If you don't find her, someone else will. And there's no guarantee that they will treat the mermaid as well as we will."

"I suppose you're right," I heard my uncle reply. "It would certainly be a big boost to my research if I found her."

"Then you'll do it?" asked Mr Showalter eagerly.

Say yes, Dr D! I thought. Say yes!

I pressed my whole body against the door.

"Yes," my uncle answered. "If there really is a mermaid, I'll find her."

Excellent! I thought.

"Very good," said Ms Wickman.

"Excellent decision," Mr Showalter added enthusiastically. "I knew we had come to the right man for the job."

"We'll be back in a couple of days to see how the search is going. I hope you'll have some good news by then," Ms Wickman said.

"That's not much time," I heard Alexander remark.

"We know," Ms Wickman replied. "But, obviously, the sooner you find her, the better."

"And, please," Mr Showalter said, "*please* keep this a secret. No one must know about the mermaid. I'm sure you can imagine what would happen if—"

CRASSSSSSSH!

I lost my balance. I fell against the door.

To my shock, it swung open—and I tumbled into the room.

I landed in a heap in the centre of the cabin floor.

Dr D, Mr Showalter, Ms Wickman and Alexander all gaped at me with their mouths open. I guess they hadn't expected me to drop in.

"Uh . . . hi, everyone," I murmured. I felt my face burning, and knew that I was blushing. "Nice day for a mermaid hunt."

Mr Showalter jumped to his feet angrily. He glared at my uncle. "This was supposed to be a secret!"

Alexander strode across the room and helped me to my feet. "Don't worry about Billy," he said. He put a protective arm around me. "You can trust him."

"I'm very embarrassed," Dr D told his visitors. "This is my nephew, Billy Deep. He and his sister are visiting me for a few weeks."

"Can they keep our secret?" asked Ms Wickman.

Dr D turned his gaze on Alexander. Alexander nodded.

"Yes, I'm sure they can," said Dr D. "Billy won't say anything to anyone. Right, Billy?"

He narrowed his eyes at me. I really do hate it when he does that. But this time I couldn't blame him.

I shook my head. "No. I won't tell anyone. I swear."

"Just to be on the safe side, Billy," said Dr D, "don't mention the mermaid to Sheena. She's too young to have to keep a big secret like this."

"I promise," I replied solemnly. I raised my right hand as if swearing an oath. "I won't breathe a word to Sheena."

This was so *cool*!

I knew the biggest secret in the world—and Sheena wouldn't have a clue!

The man and woman from the zoo exchanged glances. I could see they were still worried.

Alexander said, "You really can trust Billy. He's very serious for someone his age."

You *bet* I'm serious, I thought.

I'm William Deep, Jr., world-famous mermaid catcher.

Mr Showalter and Ms Wickman seemed to relax a little.

"Good," said Ms Wickman. She shook hands with Dr D, Alexander and me.

Mr Showalter gathered up some papers and put them into the briefcase.

"We'll see you in a few days, then," said Ms Wickman. "Good luck."

I won't need luck, I thought, watching them roar away on their boat a few minutes later.

I won't need luck because I have skill. And daring.

My head spun with all kinds of exciting thoughts.

Would I let Sheena be on TV with me after I single-handedly captured the mermaid?

Probably not.

That night I sneaked off the boat and slipped into the dark water. I swam noiselessly towards the lagoon.

I glanced back at the *Cassandra*. It floated quietly. All the portholes were dark.

Good, I thought. No one is awake to notice that I'm gone. No one knows I'm out here. No one knows I'm swimming in the sea at night, all alone.

Swimming steadily, easily, under the silvery moonlight, I made my way around the reef and into the dark lagoon.

I slowed my stroke just past the reef.

My eyes darted eagerly around the lagoon. The waves lapped gently under me. The water sparkled as if a million tiny diamonds floated on the surface.

Where was the mermaid?

I knew she was there. I knew I would find her here.

From deep below me, I heard a low rumble.

I listened hard. The sound, faint at first, grew louder.

The waves tossed as the sound became a steady roar.

It rumbled like an earthquake. An earthquake on the ocean floor.

The waves tumbled and tossed. I struggled to stay on top of them.

What was happening?

Suddenly, from the middle of the lagoon, a huge wave swelled. It rose higher, like a gigantic geyser.

Higher. Over my head. As tall as a building!

A tidal wave?

No.

The wave broke.

The dark creature pushed up underneath it.

Water slid off its grotesque body. Its single eye stared out darkly at me. Its tentacles writhed and stretched.

I screamed.

The monster blinked its muddy brown eye at me.

I tried to turn and swim away.

But it was too fast.

The tentacles whipped out—and grabbed me, tightening, tightening around my waist.

Then a slimy, cold tentacle wrapped around my neck and started to squeeze.

"I—I can't breathe!" I managed to choke out.

I tugged at the tentacle twining around my throat.

"Help me—somebody!"

I opened my eyes—and stared up at the ceiling.

I was lying in bed.

In my cabin.

The sheet was wrapped tightly around me.

I took a deep breath and waited for my heart to stop thudding. A dream.

Only a dream.

I rubbed my eyes, lifted myself, and peered out of the porthole. The sun was just rising over the horizon. The sky was morning red. The water a hazy purple.

Squinting past the reef, I saw the lagoon. Perfectly still. Not a sea monster in sight.

I wiped the sweat from my forehead with my pyjama sleeve.

No need to be afraid, I told myself. It was just a dream. A bad dream.

I shook my head, trying to forget about the sea monster.

I couldn't let it scare me. I couldn't let it stop me from finding that mermaid.

Was anyone up? Had I yelled out loud in my sleep?

I listened carefully. I could hear only the creaking of the boat, the splash of waves against its side.

The pink morning sunlight cheered me. The dark water looked inviting.

I slipped into my swimming trunks and crept out of my cabin as quietly as I could. I didn't want anyone to hear me.

In the galley I saw a half-empty pot of coffee sitting on the warmer. That meant Dr D was already up.

I tiptoed down the passageway and listened. I could hear him pottering around in the main lab.

I grabbed my snorkel, flippers and mask, and went up on deck. Nobody up there.

The coast was clear.

Silently, I climbed down the ladder, slipped into the water, and snorkelled towards the lagoon.

I know it was crazy to sneak away like that. But you can't imagine how excited I was. Even in my wildest daydreams as William Deep, Jr., undersea explorer, I never thought I would see a real, live mermaid!

As I snorkelled towards the lagoon, I tried to imagine what she would look like.

Mr Showalter had said she looked like a young girl with long, blonde hair and a green fish tail.

Weird, I thought.

Half-human, half-fish.

I tried to imagine my own legs replaced by a fish tail.

I'd be the greatest swimmer on Earth if I had a fish tail, I thought. I could win the Olympics without even practising.

I wonder if she's pretty? I thought. And I wonder if she can talk? I hope she can. She can tell me all kinds of secrets of the oceans.

I wonder how she breathes underwater?

I wonder if she thinks like a human or like a fish?

So many questions.

This is going to be the greatest adventure of my life, I thought. After I'm famous, I'll write a book about my undersea adventures. I'll call it *Courage of the Deep*, by William Deep, Jr. Maybe someone will even turn it into a film.

I raised my head and saw that I was nearing the reef. I concentrated on keeping away from it. I didn't want to touch that fire coral again.

I couldn't wait to explore the lagoon. I was so excited, I forgot all about the terrifying dream I had had the night before.

I kicked my legs carefully, watching out for red coral.

I was nearly past the reef when I felt something brush my leg.

"Oh!" I cried out and swallowed a mouthful of salty water.

Sputtering and choking, I felt something wrap around my ankle.

As it grabbed at me, it scratched my ankle.

This time I knew for sure it wasn't seaweed.

Seaweed doesn't have claws!

Ignoring the panic that nearly froze me, I kicked
and thrashed with all my strength.

"Stop it! Stop kicking me!" a voice screamed.

The mermaid?

"Hey—!" I cried out angrily as Sheena's head
appeared beside me.

She pulled up her snorkelling mask. "I didn't
scratch you *that* hard!" she snapped. "You don't
have to go crazy!"

"What are *you* doing here?" I cried.

"What are *you* doing here?" she demanded
nastily. "You know Dr D told us not to swim
here."

"Then you shouldn't be here—*should* you?" I
shouted.

"I knew you were up to something, so I
followed you," Sheena replied, adjusting her
mask.

"I'm not up to anything," I lied. "I'm just
snorkelling."

"Sure, Billy. You're just snorkelling at six-thirty in the morning exactly where you're not supposed to—*and* where you burned your foot on that fire coral yesterday. You're either up to something, or you're totally crazy!" She squinted at me, waiting for a response.

What a choice! I was either up to something, or crazy. Which should I admit to?

If I admitted I was up to something, I'd have to tell her about the mermaid—and I couldn't do that.

"Okay," I said with a casual shrug. "I guess I'm crazy."

"Well, big news," she muttered sarcastically. "Come on back to the boat, Billy," said Sheena. "Dr D will be looking for us."

"You go back. I'll be there in a little while."

"Billy," said Sheena. "Dr D is going to be very mad. He's probably ready to hop in the dinghy and search for us right now."

I was about to give up and go with her. Then, out of the corner of my eye, I saw a big splash on the other side of the reef.

The mermaid! I thought. That's got to be her! If I don't go and look for her now, I might miss her!

I turned away from Sheena and started swimming very fast, straight for the reef.

I could hear Sheena screaming, "Billy! Come back! *Billy!*"

I thought I heard an extra note of panic in her voice, but I ignored it. Just Sheena trying to scare me again, I thought.

"*Billy!*" she screamed again. "*Billy!*"

I kept on swimming.

No way I was going to stop now.

But as it turned out, I should have listened to her.

Swimming fast, I raised my head, searching for a good place to swim safely over the fire coral.

I saw another splash. Across the lagoon. Near the shore.

That's *got* to be the mermaid! I thought excitedly.

I stared hard, trying to catch a glimpse of her.

I thought I saw some kind of fin.

I made my way past the reef into the deep, still waters of the lagoon. I strained to see the mermaid, but my mask had fogged.

Rats! I thought. What a time for my mask to start leaking!

I came up for air and pulled off the mask. I hoped I wouldn't lose sight of the mermaid because of this.

I wiped the water from my eyes and, leaving the mask wrapped around my wrist, stared towards the lagoon.

That's when I saw it. A few hundred yards away.

Not the green fish tail of a mermaid.

The fin I saw was a grey-white triangle sticking straight up in the water.

The fin of a hammerhead shark.

As I stared in horror, the fin turned in the water, and then ripped towards me, moving steady and straight as a torpedo.

Where was Sheena?

Was she still behind me?

I glanced back. I could see her in the distance, splashing back to the boat.

I was forced to forget about Sheena as the grey fin swiftly moved closer.

I thrashed my arms in the water, trying to swim away.

When the shark swam right past me, I stopped thrashing.

Would it go away? Would it leave me alone?

My heart in my throat, I started swimming in the other direction, towards the reef. Away from the shark.

I kept my eyes on that fin.

It began to turn. The shark's fin streamed towards me in a wide arc.

"Ohhh." I let out a terrified groan as I realized it was circling me.

Now I didn't know which way to go. The shark

swam between me and the boat. If I could turn around and climb on to the reef, maybe I would be safe.

The huge fin slid closer.

I plunged towards the reef. I knew I had to keep distance between me and the shark.

Suddenly, the fin shot up in front of me—between me and the reef.

The shark kept circling, closing in, swimming faster and faster, making the circle smaller as he swam.

I was trapped. But I couldn't stay still. I couldn't just float there, waiting for the shark to eat me.

I had to fight. I kicked my legs in a panic as I swam towards the reef.

I was nearer to the reef now. But the shark's circles grew smaller, smaller.

I breathed in quick, shallow gasps. I couldn't think clearly. I was too terrified. The same two words echoed in my brain: *The shark. The shark.*

Over and over again. *The shark. The shark.*

The shark swam around me in a tight circle. His tail swished, sending up waves of water over me.

The shark. The shark.

I stared at the monster in wide-eyed horror. He swam so close, I could see him clearly. He was big—at least ten feet long. His head was wide and hideous, long like the head of a hammer, with an eye on each end.

I heard my voice quivering, "No . . . no . . ."

Something cold brushed my leg.

The shark. The shark.

My stomach lurched. I threw my head back and let out a howl of sheer terror.

"Aaaaaiiii!"

Pain jolted down my spine.

The shark had bumped me with its snout. My body rose out of the water, then hit the surface with a *smack*.

I froze.

The shark was hungry.

It wanted to fight.

It circled me again, then zoomed straight for me.

Its jaws opened. I saw rows and rows of sharp teeth.

I screamed out a hoarse, "NO!" I thrashed, panicked. I kicked with all my strength.

The razor teeth brushed by, just missing my leg.

The reef. I had to get to the reef. It was my only chance.

I dived for the coral. The shark plunged towards me. I dodged it once more.

I grabbed the red coral. Pain shot through my hand. The fire coral.

I didn't care.

174

The top of the reef sat just above the surface of the water. I tried to pull myself up. My whole body stung.

I had almost made it. Soon I'd be safe.

With a mighty kick, I hoisted myself on to the reef—and was yanked back into the water.

My stomach slammed against the side of the reef. I felt a sharp stab of pain in my leg.

I tried to pull my leg away. I couldn't.

It was caught in the jaws of the shark.

My mind screamed with terror.

The shark. The shark.

It's got me!

My entire body burned with pain. I slipped heavily into the water.

The shark knew he had me. I had no strength left to fight.

Then something splashed nearby.

The shark released my leg and jerked towards the splash.

I had no time to catch my breath. The shark circled back. It charged at me.

The gaping jaws moved in for the kill.

I shut my eyes and let out a shrill scream of terror.

A second passed. Then another.

Nothing happened.

I heard a loud thump.

I opened my eyes.

Something had come between me and the shark, a few feet in front of me.

I stared. The water churned white. A long, shiny green fish tail rose out of the water and splashed back down.

Another fish was fighting the shark!

The shark rolled over, then attacked. The green fish tail smacked the shark hard. The shark went under.

I couldn't see what was happening. The water rocked higher, tossing up frothy, white waves.

All around me the water bubbled and churned, white with foam. Over the crash of the water, I heard shrill animal squeals.

Sharks don't squeal, do they? I thought. What is making that sound?

The shark surfaced, its toothy jaws gaping. It snapped them at something, once, twice. Snapping at air.

The long, green fish tail rose out of the water and smacked the shark hard. A direct hit on its broad hammerhead.

The shark shut its jaws and sank below the surface.

Then I heard a loud *bump*! The water stopped churning.

A second later, the huge grey fin surfaced a few yards away, speeding off in the other direction.

The shark was swimming away!

I stared at the green fish tail as it arced over the dark, swelling water.

As the waters calmed, I heard a low, musical

sound. It was beautiful and slightly sad. Whistling and humming at the same time.

It sounded something like a whale. But this creature was much smaller than a whale.

The green tail swung round. Then the creature lifted its head.

A head with long, blonde hair.

The mermaid!

178

Bobbing in the water, I forgot my burning pain as I gaped at her.

To my amazement, the mermaid looked just as the zoo people had said she would.

Her head and shoulders were smaller than mine, but her flashing green tail stretched out, long and powerful. Her wide, sea-green eyes sparkled. Her skin gave off a pale pink glow.

I stared at her, unable to speak.

She's real! I thought. And she's so beautiful!

At last I found my voice. "You—you saved me," I stammered. "You saved my life. Thank you!"

She shyly lowered her eyes and cooed at me through shell-pink lips. What was she trying to say?

"What can I do in return?" I asked her. "I'll do anything I can."

She smiled, and uttered that haunting low

hum. She was trying to talk to me. I wished I could understand her.

She reached for my hand and examined it, frowning over the red burns from the fire coral. Her hand felt cool. She passed it over the palm of my hand, and the pain from the burns began to fade away.

"Wow!" I exclaimed. I must have sounded pretty stupid, but I didn't know what else to say. Her touch was like magic. When she held my hand, I could float without treading water. Just as she did.

Was this another dream?

I closed my eyes and opened them again.

I was still floating in the sea, staring at a blonde-haired mermaid.

No. Not a dream.

She smiled again and shook her head, making those low singing sounds.

I could hardly believe that only a few minutes before I'd been frantically fighting off a hungry shark.

I raised my head and searched the waters. The shark had vanished. The water had calmed, shimmering like gold now under the morning sunlight. And there I was, floating in the sea off a deserted island with a real mermaid.

Sheena will never believe this, I thought. Not in a million years.

Suddenly, the mermaid flipped her tail and disappeared under the water.

Startled, I searched around for her. She had left without a trace—not a ripple, not a bubble.

Where did she go? I wondered. Is she gone, just like that? Will I never see her again?

I rubbed my eyes and looked for her again. No sign of her. A few fish darted past me.

She had disappeared so instantly, I began to think I had dreamed her up after all.

Just then, I felt a tiny pinch on my foot.

"Ouch!" I yelled, quickly pulling away. I began to panic. The shark was back!

Then, behind me, I heard a small splash and a whistle-like giggle. I turned round.

The mermaid smiled mischievously at me. She snapped her fingers in a pinching motion.

"It was you!" I cried, laughing with relief. "You're worse than my little sister!"

She whistled again and slapped her tail against the surface of the water.

Suddenly, a dark shadow fell across her face. I raised my eyes to see what it was.

Too late.

A heavy net dropped over us. Startled, I thrashed my arms and legs. But that only tangled them more in the rope.

The net tightened over both of us. We were thrown together.

We struggled helplessly as the net jerked us up.

The mermaid's eyes widened and she squealed in terror.

"EEEEE!" she cried.

We were being pulled up out of the water.

"EEEEEE!" The mermaid's frightened wail rose like a siren, drowning out my feeble cries for help.

"Billy—I don't believe it!"

I gazed up through the holes in the net and recognized Dr D and Sheena. They struggled to pull us aboard the dinghy.

Sheena stared down at me and the mermaid in amazement. Dr D's eyes were wide, and his mouth hung open.

"You've found her, Billy!" he said. "You've actually found the mermaid!"

"Just get me out of this net!" I cried. Somehow, I didn't feel so great about capturing the mermaid any more.

"The zoo people were right," Dr D muttered to himself. "It's unbelievable. It's astounding. It's historic . . ."

We landed in a heap on the floor of the dinghy. The mermaid squirmed beside me in the net, making sharp, angry, clicking noises.

Dr D watched her closely. He touched her tail.

183

The mermaid flapped it hard against the bottom of the boat.

"Is there any way this could be a hoax?" he wondered aloud.

"Billy—is this one of your stupid tricks?" Sheena demanded suspiciously.

"It's not a trick," I said. "Now will you get me out of this net? The ropes are digging into my skin."

They ignored me.

Sheena gently reached one finger through the net and touched the scales on the mermaid's tail. "I can't believe it," she murmured. "She's really real!"

"Of course she's real!" I cried. "We're both real, and we're both very uncomfortable!"

"Well, it's hard to believe anything *you* say," Sheena snapped. "After all, you've been talking about sea monsters ever since we got here."

"I *did* see a sea monster!" I cried.

"Quiet, kids," said Dr D. "Let's get our discovery back to the sea lab."

He started the dinghy's motor and we roared back to the big boat.

Alexander stood on deck, waiting for us. "It's really true!" he cried excitedly. "It's really a mermaid!"

Sheena tied the dinghy to the side of the *Cassandra* while Dr D and Alexander hoisted me and the mermaid aboard.

Dr D opened the net and helped me out. The mermaid flopped her tail and got herself even more tangled in the net.

Alexander shook my hand. "I'm proud of you, Billy. How did you do it? This is amazing." He gave me a vigorous pat on the back. "Do you realize this is the greatest ocean find of the century? Maybe of all time?"

"Thanks," I said. "But I didn't do anything. I didn't find her—*she* found *me*."

The mermaid flopped violently on deck. Her squeals became higher-pitched, more frantic.

Alexander's face fell. "We've got to do something for her," he said urgently.

"Dr D, you've got to let her go," I said. "She needs to be in the water."

"I'll fill the big tank with seawater, Dr D," said Alexander. He hurried off to fill the tank.

"We can't let her go just yet, Billy," said Dr D. "Not without examining her first." His eyes were shining with excitement. But he saw how upset I was. "We won't hurt her, Billy. She'll be all right."

His eyes dropped to my leg, and he frowned. He kneeled down to look at it.

"You're bleeding, Billy," he said. "Are you okay?"

"I'm fine," I said. "But the mermaid isn't."

He ignored me.

"How did this happen?" asked Dr D.

"A shark grabbed my leg," I told him. "Just as he was about to clamp down, the mermaid came. She saved my life. You should have seen her fighting that shark."

Dr D turned to the mermaid as if seeing her for the first time.

"Wow," said Sheena. "She fought off a shark? All by herself?"

The mermaid's long green tail pounded angrily on the deck of the boat.

"EEEEE! EEEEEE!" she cried shrilly. She almost sounded as if she were screaming.

"Forget about my leg," I shouted. "You've got to let the mermaid go!"

Dr D stood up, shaking his head. "Billy, I'm a scientist. This mermaid is an extremely important discovery. If I let her go, I'd be letting down the entire scientific community. I'd be letting down the entire world!"

"You just want the million pounds," I muttered.

I knew it was cruel, but I couldn't stop myself. I hated seeing the mermaid so unhappy.

Dr D looked hurt.

"That's not fair, Billy," he said. "I think you know me better than that."

I avoided his gaze. Lowering my head, I pretended to examine the cut on my leg. It wasn't very deep. Alexander had given me some gauze. I pressed it against the cut.

"I only want the money to continue my research," Dr D went on. "I would never use this mermaid to get rich."

That was true. I knew Dr D didn't care about the money for himself. All he wanted was to keep on studying fish.

"Just think about it, Billy. You've found a mermaid! A creature we all thought didn't exist! We can't just let her go. We've got to find out a little bit about her," he said excitedly.

I said nothing.

"We won't hurt her, Billy, I promise."

Alexander returned. "The tank is ready, Dr D."

"Thanks." Dr D followed him to the other side of the boat.

I glanced at Sheena to see whose side she was on. Did she want to keep the mermaid? Or let her go?

But Sheena just stood there, watching. Her face was tense. I could tell she wasn't sure which of us were right.

But when I looked at the mermaid, I knew *I* was right.

She had finally stopped squirming and flipping her tail. Now she lay still on the deck, the net draped over her. She was breathing hard and staring out at the ocean with watery, sad eyes.

I wished I'd never tried to find her in the first

187

place. Now all I wanted was to find some way to help her get back to her home.

Dr D and Alexander came back. They lifted the mermaid inside the net. Alexander lifted her tail, and Dr D held her head.

"Don't squirm, little mermaid," Dr D said in a soothing voice. "Keep still."

The mermaid seemed to understand. She didn't flop around. But her eyes rolled wildly, and she uttered low moans.

Dr D and Alexander carried her to the giant glass tank. It stood on the deck now, full of fresh seawater. They gently dropped her into the tank, pulling the net away as she slid into the water. Then they put a screen top over the tank and clamped it shut.

The mermaid churned the water with her tail. Then, gradually, her tail stopped moving. She grew still.

Her body slumped lifelessly to the bottom of the tank.

She didn't move or breathe.

"Noooo!" An angry cry escaped my lips. "She's dead! She's dead! We've *killed* her!"

Sheena had moved to the other side of the tank. "Billy, look—!" she called to me.

I hurried round to her.

"The mermaid isn't dead," Sheena reported, pointing. "Look. She—she's crying or something."

My sister was right. The mermaid had slumped to the bottom of the tank and had buried her face in her hands. "Now what do we do?" I asked.

No one answered.

"We have to find a method of feeding her," my uncle said, rubbing his chin, his eyes on the tank.

"Do you think she eats like a person or a fish?" I asked.

"If only she could tell us," said Alexander. "She can't talk, can she, Billy?"

"I don't think so," I said. "She just makes sounds. Whistles and clicks and hums."

"I'll go down to the lab and get some equipment ready," said Alexander. "Maybe we can find out something about her with the sonar monitor."

"Good idea," said Dr D thoughtfully.

Alexander hurried below.

"I think I'd better go to Santa Anita for some supplies," said Dr D. Santa Anita was the nearest inhabited island. "I'll buy lots of different kinds of foods. We can try them out on her until we find something she likes. Would you two like anything while I'm there?"

"How about some peanut butter?" Sheena asked quickly. "There's no way Alexander can ruin a peanut butter sandwich!"

Dr D nodded as he climbed into the dinghy. "Peanut butter it is. Anything else? Billy?"

I shook my head.

"All right," Dr D said. "I'll be back in a few hours."

He started the motor, and the dinghy sped off towards Santa Anita.

"It's so hot," Sheena complained. "I'm going down to my cabin for a while."

"Okay," I said, my eyes on the mermaid.

It *was* hot up on deck. There was no breeze, and the white-hot noon sun beat down on my face.

But I couldn't go below deck. I couldn't leave the mermaid.

She floated behind the glass, her long tail drooping. When she saw me, she pressed her hands and face to the glass and cooed sadly.

I waved to her through the glass.

She cooed and hummed in her low voice, trying to communicate with me. I listened, trying to understand.

"Are you hungry?" I asked her.

She stared at me blankly.

"Are you hungry?" I repeated, rubbing my stomach. "Go like this—" I nodded my head up and down—"for yes. Do this for no." I shook my head back and forth.

I stopped and waited to see what she'd do.

She nodded her head yes.

"Yes?" I said. "You *are* hungry?"

She shook her head no.

"No? You're not hungry?"

She nodded her head yes. Then she shook her head no again.

She's just copying me, I thought. She doesn't really understand.

I took a step back and studied her in the tank.

She's young, I thought. She's a lot like me. That means she *must* be hungry. And she probably likes to eat what I like. Right?

Maybe. It was worth a try.

I hurried down to the galley. I pulled open a cupboard and took out a package of chocolate chip cookies.

191

Okay, so it's not exactly seafood, I thought. But who wouldn't like chocolate chip cookies?

I grabbed a few cookies and stuffed the package back in the cupboard. Alexander came through on his way up to the deck. He was carrying some equipment in his arms.

"Getting a snack?" he asked me.

"For the mermaid," I told him. "Do you think she'll like them?"

He shrugged his broad shoulders and said, "Who knows?"

He followed me out on deck, carrying the equipment.

"What's all that stuff?" I asked him.

"I thought we could run a few tests on the mermaid, to see what we can find out about her," said Alexander. "But go ahead and feed her first."

"Okay," I said. "Here goes."

I held a cookie up to the glass. The mermaid stared at it. I could see that she didn't know what it was.

"Mmmmm," I said, patting my stomach. "Yummy."

The mermaid patted her tummy, imitating me. She stared out at me blankly with those sea-green eyes.

Alexander reached up and unlatched the screen top. I handed him the cookie, and he dropped it into the tank.

The mermaid watched it falling towards her through the water. She made no attempt to grab it.

By the time it reached her, it was soggy. It fell apart in the tank.

"Yuck," I said. "Even I wouldn't eat it now."

The mermaid pushed the soggy cookie pieces away.

"Maybe Dr D will have something she likes when he gets back," said Alexander.

"I hope so," I said.

Alexander began to set up his equipment. He put a thermometer inside the tank, and some long white plastic tubes.

"Oh, man," Alexander mumbled, shaking his head. "I forgot my notebook."

He hurried back down to the lab.

I watched the mermaid float sadly in her tank, with all the tubes coming out of it. She reminded me of the fish down in the lab.

No, I thought. She's not a fish. She shouldn't be treated this way.

I remembered how she had fought the shark.

She could have been killed, I thought. Easily. But she fought the shark, anyway, just to help me.

The mermaid cooed. Then I saw her wipe away the tears that had begun to run down her face.

She's crying again, I thought, feeling guilty and miserable. She's pleading with me. I put my face against the glass, as close to hers as I could get it.

I've got to help her, I thought.

I put a finger to my lips. "Sshhh," I whispered. "Stay quiet. I have to work quickly!"

I knew I was about to do something that would make Dr D very angry.

My uncle would probably never forgive me.

But I didn't care.

I was going to do what I thought was right.

I was going to set the mermaid free.

My hand trembled as I reached up to unlatch the screen at the top of the tank. The tank was taller than I was. I wasn't quite sure how I'd get the mermaid out of there. But I had to find a way.

As I struggled to pull the screen off, the mermaid began to squeal, "Eeee! EEEEEE!"

"Sshh! Don't make any noise!" I warned her.

Then I felt a hand grab me by the arm. I gasped, startled.

A deep voice asked, "What are you doing?"

I turned round to see Alexander standing behind me.

I stepped away from the tank, and he let go of my arm.

"Billy, what were you doing?" he asked again.

"I was going to let her go!" I cried. "Alexander, you can't keep her in there! Look how unhappy she is!"

We both stared at the mermaid, who had slumped to the bottom of the tank again. I think she knew that I had tried to help her—and that I had been stopped.

I caught the sadness on Alexander's face. I could tell he felt sorry for her. But he had a job to do.

He turned to me and put an arm around my shoulders. "Billy, you've got to understand how important this mermaid is to your uncle," he said. "He's worked his whole life for a discovery like this. It would break his heart if you let her go."

He slowly led me away from the tank. I turned back to look at the mermaid again.

"But what about *her* heart?" I asked. "I think it's breaking her heart to be stuck in that fish tank."

Alexander sighed. "It's not ideal, I know that. But it's only temporary. Soon she'll have plenty of room to swim and play in."

Sure, I thought bitterly. As an exhibit at the zoo, with millions of people gawking at her every day.

Alexander removed his arm from my shoulders and rubbed his chin.

"Your uncle is a very caring man, Billy," he said. "He'll do his best to make sure the mermaid has everything she needs. But it's his duty to study her. The things he can learn from her could help people understand the oceans better—and take better care of them. That's important, right?"

"I guess so," I said.

I knew Alexander had a good point. I loved Dr D, and I didn't want to spoil his big discovery.

But, still, the mermaid shouldn't have to suffer for science, I thought.

"Come on, Billy," Alexander said, leading me below deck. "I promised you I'd show you how the sonar probes work, didn't I? Let's go down to the lab, and I'll give you a demonstration."

As we started to climb below, I took one last glance back at the mermaid. She was still slumped forlornly at the bottom of the tank. Her head was lowered, her blonde hair floating limply above it like seaweed.

The sonar probes weren't as interesting as I thought they'd be. All they did was beep whenever the *Cassandra* was in danger of running ashore.

I guess Alexander could tell my mind was not on the sonar probes. "Want some lunch?" he asked me.

Uh-oh. Lunch. I was hungry. But not for spicy chicken salad.

I hesitated. "Well, I had a big breakfast . . ."

"I'll whip up something special," Alexander

offered. "We can have a picnic up on deck with the mermaid. Come on."

What could I do? I followed him to the kitchen.

He opened the small refrigerator and pulled out a bowl.

"This has been marinating all morning," he said.

I looked into the bowl. It was full of thin strips of something white and rubbery-looking. They floated in an oily, dark grey liquid.

Whatever it was, I knew I couldn't eat it.

"It's marinated squid," said Alexander. "I added some squid ink for extra flavour. That's what makes it grey."

"Yum," I said, rolling my eyes. "I haven't had squid ink in days!"

"Don't be so sarcastic. You might be surprised," Alexander replied. He handed me the bowl. "Take this up on deck. I'll bring some bread and iced tea."

I carried the bowl of squid up and set it down near the mermaid's tank.

"How are you doing, Mermaid?" I asked her.

She flipped her tail a little. Then she opened and closed her mouth, as if she were chewing.

"Hey," I said. "You *are* hungry, aren't you?"

She kept making that chewing motion. I glanced down at the bowl of squid.

Who knows? I thought. This might be just what she'd like.

198

I stood on a rail and unlatched the top of the tank. Then I dropped in a piece of the rubbery squid.

The mermaid leaped towards it and caught it in her mouth.

She chewed, then smiled.

She liked it!

I gave her some more. She ate it.

I rubbed my stomach. "Do you like it?" I asked her. I nodded yes.

She smiled again. Then she nodded yes.

She understood me!

"What are you doing, Billy?" Alexander asked. He had come up on deck carrying two plates and a loaf of bread.

"Alexander, look!" I cried. "We communicated!"

I dropped another piece of squid into the tank. She ate it. Then she nodded yes.

"That means she likes it!" I said.

"Wow," murmured Alexander. He put down the plates and picked up his notebook. He scribbled some notes.

"Isn't that fantastic?" I demanded. "I'm a scientist, too—aren't I, Alexander?"

He nodded, but kept writing.

"I mean, I'm the first person on Earth to communicate with a mermaid—right?" I insisted.

"If she stays with us long enough, you might

be able to talk to her in sign language," he said. "Just think of the things we could learn!"

He spoke aloud as he wrote, "Likes to eat squid." Then he put down his pencil and said, "Hey, wait! That's our lunch!"

Uh-oh, I thought. I hope his feelings aren't hurt.

He looked at me. He looked at the bowl. He looked at the mermaid.

Then he started laughing.

"At least *somebody* around here likes my cooking!" he exclaimed.

About an hour later, Dr D returned with the shopping. Luckily he had bought plenty of seafood in Santa Anita. We fed some of it to the mermaid for supper. While she ate, Dr D checked the readings on the meters Alexander had set up in the tank.

"Interesting," Dr D commented. "She sends out sonar signals through the water. Just as whales do."

"What does that mean?" asked Sheena.

"It means there are probably other mermaids like her," said Dr D. "She must be trying to contact them with underwater sounds."

Poor mermaid, I thought. She's calling to her friends. She wants to be rescued.

I went to my cabin after supper and stared

out of the little porthole.

An orange sun sank slowly into the purple horizon. A wide carpet of gold light shimmered in the rolling ocean waters. A cool breeze blew in through the porthole.

I watched the sun drop into the ocean. The sky immediately darkened, as if someone had turned off a lamp.

The mermaid is up there all alone, I thought. She must be so frightened. A prisoner. Trapped in a fish tank in the dark.

The door to my cabin suddenly burst open. Sheena bounded in, panting, her eyes wide.

"Sheena!" I scolded angrily. "How many times do I have to tell you to knock first?"

She ignored me. "But, Billy!" she gasped. "She's escaped! The mermaid's escaped!"

201

I leaped off my bed, my heart pounding.

"She's not there!" Sheena cried. "She's not in her tank!"

I darted out of the cabin, up the hatch, and out on deck.

Part of me hoped she really had escaped to freedom. But part of me wished she could stay for ever—and make my uncle the most famous scientist in the world and me the most famous nephew of a scientist!

Please let her be okay, I thought.

Up on deck, my eyes adjusted to the evening darkness. Tiny lights glowed all around the edge of the boat.

I squinted across the deck at the giant fish tank.

I ran so fast, I nearly toppled overboard. Sheena was right behind me.

"Hey—!" I cried out when I saw the mermaid floating listlessly in the water, her green tail shimmering faintly in the fading light.

It took me a few seconds to realize that Sheena was laughing. "Gotcha!" she shouted gleefully. "Gotcha again, Billy!"

I groaned long and loud. Another one of Sheena's stupid tricks.

"Good one, Sheena," I said bitterly. "Very clever."

"You're just mad because I fooled you again. You're so easy to trick."

The mermaid raised her eyes to me, and a faint smile formed on her pale lips. "Looorrrooo, looorrrooo," she cooed at me.

"She really is pretty," Sheena said.

The mermaid is hoping I'll let her go now, I thought. Maybe I should. . .

Sheena could help me, I decided. It would be easier with the two of us.

But would my sister cooperate? "Sheena—" I began.

I heard footsteps behind us. "Hey, kids." It was Dr D. "It's almost bedtime," he called. "Ready to go below?"

"We never go to bed this early at home," Sheena whined.

"Maybe not. But I bet you don't get up so early at home, either. Do you?"

Sheena shook her head. We all stood at the tank and watched the mermaid in silence. She gave her tail a little flick and settled back down at the bottom of the tank.

"Don't worry about her," Dr D said. "I'll check on her during the night to make sure she's all right."

The mermaid pressed her tiny hands against the glass wall of the tank. Her eyes pleaded with us, pleaded with us to set her free.

"She'll feel better once she gets to Marina Zoo," Dr D said. "They're building a special lagoon just for her, with a reef and everything. It'll be exactly like the lagoon off Ilandra. She'll be free to swim and play. She'll feel at home."

I hope so, I thought. But I didn't feel so sure.

The *Cassandra* rocked gently on the waves that night, but I couldn't fall asleep.

I lay on my bunk, staring at the ceiling. A pale beam of moonlight fell through the porthole and across my face. I couldn't stop thinking about the mermaid.

I tried to imagine what it would feel like to be trapped in a glass tank for a whole day. It probably wouldn't be that different from being trapped in this tiny cabin, I thought, glancing around. My cabin was about as big as a cupboard.

It would be terrible, I thought, fiddling with the collar of my pyjama top. I pushed open the porthole to let in more air.

The fish tank might not even be the worst of it,

I figured. I know Dr D cares about the mermaid. I know he'd never hurt her.

But what will happen to her when the zoo people take her away? Who will look out for her?

Sure, they're building a fancy fake lagoon. But it won't be the same as the real lagoon. And there will be people around, staring at her all the time. They'll probably expect her to perform tricks or something; maybe jump through hoops like a trained seal.

They'll probably put her in TV commercials, too. And TV shows and movies.

She'll be a prisoner. A lonely prisoner for the rest of her life.

This is all my fault. How could I let this happen?

I have to do something, I decided. I can't let them take her.

Just then I thought I heard something—a low hum. I lay very still and listened. At first I thought it was the mermaid. But I quickly realized it was a motor.

I heard it chugging softly, from a distance. But slowly the sound moved closer.

A boat.

I sat up and peered out of the porthole. A large boat pulled quietly up beside the *Cassandra*.

Who was it? The zoo people?

In the middle of the night?

No. It wasn't the same boat. This boat was much bigger.

As I peered out of the small porthole, I saw two dark figures quietly slip on board the *Cassandra*. Then two more.

My heart began to race. Who *are* these people? I wondered. What are they doing?

What should I do?

Should I sneak up and spy on them? What if they see me?

Then I heard more strange noises.

A thud. A muffled cry of pain.

It came from the deck.

The deck. Where the mermaid was trapped helplessly in her tank.

Oh, no! I thought, feeling a chill of panic. They're hurting the mermaid!

I charged up to the deck. Sheena ran right behind me.

Stumbling over a tow rope, I grabbed the rail to steady myself. Then I darted blindly to the fish tank.

The mermaid was huddled up at the bottom of the tank, her arms wrapped protectively around herself.

I saw four men standing tensely near the tank. All four were dressed in black. They had black masks pulled over their faces.

One of them held a small club in his hand.

And a body lay sprawled on the deck, face down.

Dr D!

Sheena screamed and ran to our uncle. She knelt beside him. "They hit him on the head!" she cried. "They knocked him out!"

I gasped. "Who are you?" I demanded. "What are you doing on our boat?"

The four men ignored me.

Two of them unfolded a heavy rope net and spread it over the fish tank. Then they let it fall into the tank, draping it over the mermaid.

"Stop it!" I yelled. "What are you doing?"

"Be quiet, kid," the man with the club muttered. He raised the club menacingly.

I watched helplessly as they tightened the net around the mermaid.

They were kidnapping her!

"Eeeee! EEEEEeeee!" she squealed in terror and started to thrash her arms about, struggling to free herself from the heavy net.

"Stop it! Leave her alone!" I cried.

One of the men gave a low laugh. The other three still ignored me.

Sheena was bent over Dr D, frantically trying to wake him up. I ran to the hatch and shouted down into the cabin, "Alexander! Alexander! Help!"

Alexander was big and strong—maybe strong enough to stop these men.

I ran back to the tank. The mermaid was trapped in the net. All four men worked to lift her out of the tank. She squirmed and fought with all her strength.

"EEEEEE!" she screamed. The high-pitched squeal hurt my ears.

"Can't you get her to shut up?" one of the men cried angrily.

"Just load her on board," the one with the club replied sharply.

"Stop!" I yelled. "You can't do that!"

Then I totally lost it.

Without thinking, I dived towards the four of them. I don't know what I planned to do. I just knew I had to stop them.

One of them pushed me away easily with one hand. "Stay away—or you'll get hurt," he muttered.

"Let her go! Let the mermaid go!" I cried frantically.

"Forget about the mermaid," said the man. "You'll never see her again."

I grabbed the rail. My heart was pounding in my chest. I gasped for breath.

I couldn't stand the mermaid's terrified screams.

I couldn't let them take her—not without a fight.

She had saved my life once. Now it was my turn to save hers.

But what could I do?

They had lifted the mermaid out of the tank. Three men held her in the net.

She squirmed and thrashed like crazy, splashing water all over the deck.

I'll tackle them, I thought. I'll knock them over. Then I'll push the mermaid into the ocean and she can swim away to safety.

Lowering my head like a football player, I took a deep breath and ran right at them.

"Billy—stop!" Sheena screamed.

I crashed into one of the men holding the net, butting him hard in the stomach with my head.

To my dismay, the man hardly moved.

He grabbed me with his free hand, lifted me up off the deck, and heaved me into the fish tank.

I splashed into the warm water and came up, choking and sputtering.

Through the glass, I watched the men toss the mermaid aboard their boat. They were getting away!

I tried to scramble out of the tank, but it was too tall. I kept sliding down the wet glass, unable to reach the top.

I knew there was only one person who could stop the masked men now. Alexander.

Where was he? Hadn't he heard all the noise?

"ALEXANDER!" I shouted as loud as I could. But my voice was muffled by the glass walls of the tank.

Then, finally, he appeared on the deck. I saw his big blond head and muscular body moving towards me. At last!

"Alexander!" I cried, scrambling to stay afloat in the tank. "Stop them!"

I could hear the motor of the other boat begin to rumble. One by one, the masked men lowered themselves off our boat.

Three of them had left the *Cassandra*. Only one remained on deck.

Through the glass I watched Alexander run up to him and grab his shoulder.

Yes! I thought. Get him, Alexander! *Get him!*

I'd never seen Alexander hit anyone before. But I knew he could do it if he had to.

But Alexander didn't hit the masked man. Instead, he asked, "Is the mermaid safely on board?"

The masked man nodded.

"Good," Alexander replied. "And have you got the money for me?"

"Got it."

"All right," Alexander murmured. "Let's get out of here!"

I nearly choked on a mouthful of water.

I just couldn't *believe* that Alexander was working with the masked men. He had seemed like such a good guy.

But I knew now that he had arranged the whole thing. He had to be the one who had told them the mermaid was on board our boat.

"Alexander," I cried, "how could you?"

He stared at me through the glass. "Hey, Billy, it's just business," he said with a shrug. "The zoo was going to pay a million pounds for the mermaid. But my new bosses will pay *twenty* million!" A thin smile crossed his face. "You know arithmetic, Billy. Which would you choose?"

"You rat!" I shouted. I wanted to punch him. I struggled to get out of the tank. All I managed to do was splash a lot and get water up my nose.

Alexander followed the masked man to his boat. I pounded helplessly on the glass tank.

Then I saw Sheena stand up. Lowering my gaze to the deck, I saw that Dr D was moving.

Alexander didn't seem to notice. He stepped over Dr D's body. He didn't even care that Dr D could have been badly hurt.

I watched my uncle reach up and grab Alexander by the ankle.

"Whoa!" Alexander tripped and fell hard on to his elbows and his knees.

Sheena screamed and backed up to the rail.

Maybe there's still hope, I thought, my heart beating faster. Maybe they won't get away after all.

Alexander sat up, dazed, rubbing one elbow. "Get them!" he shouted down to the masked men.

Two of them climbed back aboard the *Cassandra* and grabbed Dr D. Sheena ran at them, flailing at them with her puny little fists.

Of course that didn't do any good. The third masked man grabbed her arms and pinned them behind her back.

"Kick them, Sheena!" I yelled through the glass.

She tried to kick the man who held her, but he just tightened his grip. She couldn't move.

"Let them go!" I screamed desperately.

"What should we do with them?" asked one of the men.

214

"Whatever you do, do it quickly," said Alexander. "We've got to get out of here."

The man who held Sheena glanced in at me. I was frantically treading water, trying to stay above the surface.

"They might call the island police or the Coast Guard," he said, frowning. "We'd better kill them."

"Throw them all in the tank!" suggested one of his partners.

"Alexander!" Dr D shouted. "I know you're not a cruel man. Don't let them do this."

Alexander avoided my uncle's hard stare. "Sorry, Dr D," he muttered. "I can't stop them. If I try to, they'll kill me, too."

Without another word, he lowered himself on to the other boat.

What a creep, I thought angrily.

Two of the masked men lifted Dr D up high and dropped him into the tank. He landed beside me with a splash.

"Are you okay?" I asked him.

He rubbed the back of his head and nodded.

Sheena was next. They tossed her in easily. She flew through the air, flailing her arms and legs. Then she plopped into the water.

The men replaced the screen lid. They clamped it shut.

I stared out at them, realizing in horror that we had no way to escape.

The water in the tank was about six feet deep. We all kicked and paddled, trying to stay above the surface. There was barely enough room for the three of us.

"All right," said one of the men. "Let's go."

"Wait!" Dr D shouted. "You can't just leave us here!"

The three men exchanged glances. "You're right. We can't," said one.

They stepped towards us.

So they aren't heartless monsters after all, I thought. They weren't going to leave us.

But what are they going to do?

The first man signalled to the other two. They raised their hands to one side of the tank.

"One, two, three—" the first man called out.

On three, they pushed the tank over the side of the deck.

We were thrown together. Then our bodies slammed against the side of the tank as it dropped into the ocean.

Ocean water seeped into the tank.

"The tank—it's sinking!" cried Dr D.

We watched the kidnappers' boat as it roared away. Our tank rocked in its wake. Then it started to sink.

"We're going under!" Sheena screamed. "We're going to drown!"

217

All three of us desperately pushed against the screen. I beat my fists against it. Dr D tried to get his shoulder against it.

But the tank tilted in the water, and we were all tossed back.

The screen was made of heavy steel mesh, and clamped on to the top of the tank. We couldn't reach the clamps from inside, so we had to try to break through it.

We pushed with all our strength. It wouldn't budge.

The tank slowly sank deeper below the surface of the dark, rolling water. The moon disappeared behind a blanket of clouds, leaving us in total darkness.

We had only a minute or two before the tank dropped completely below the surface.

Sheena started to cry. "I'm so afraid!" she shrieked. "I'm so afraid!"

Dr D pounded his fists against the glass

tank wall, trying to break through.

I ran my hands all along the top of the tank, looking for a weak spot in the screen.

Then I hit something.

A tiny latch.

"Look!" I cried, pointing to the latch.

I fumbled with it, trying to open it. "It's stuck!"

"Let me try." Dr D tore at the latch with his fingers. "It's jammed shut," he said.

Sheena took a red clip from her hair. "Maybe we can loosen it with this," she said.

Dr D took the hairclip and scraped hard around the latch.

"It's working!" he said.

Maybe there's hope, I thought. Maybe we'll get out of here!

Dr D stopped scraping and tugged at the latch.

It moved!

It opened!

"We're free!" cried Sheena.

We all pushed at the screen. We pushed again.

We pushed again. The screen didn't move. The latch hadn't opened it after all. Two other latches held the screen in place.

Two latches we couldn't reach.

We all grew silent. The only sounds now were Sheena's soft, frightened sobs and the steady wash of the waves.

The water had risen nearly to the top of the

tank. Soon it would come rushing in on us.

Suddenly, the ocean darkened. The waters grew choppy, and the tank rocked a little faster.

"What's that noise?" Sheena asked.

I listened.

Through the churning of the water, I heard a strange sound. It was very faint, as if coming from far away.

A shrill, high-pitched whistle.

"It sounds like a siren," Dr D murmured. "Lots of sirens."

The eerie wails rose and fell over the water.

Louder. Closer.

The sound—as shrill as the screech of metal—surrounded us.

Suddenly, dark, shadowy forms swirled around the tank.

We pressed our faces to the glass.

"That sound. I've never heard anything like it. What can it be?" asked Dr D.

"It—it's coming from all around!" I stammered.

The dark water tossed, churned by the shadowy forms. I peered through the foam, straining to see.

Suddenly, out of the murky water, a face appeared. It pressed itself against the glass, right in front of my face!

I gasped and pulled back.

Then I saw more faces. We were surrounded by small, girlish faces. Their wide eyes peered in at us menacingly.

"Mermaids!" I shrieked.

"Dozens of them!" Dr D murmured in hushed amazement.

They churned the water with their long tails.

Their hair, dark tangles in the black water, floated around their faces. The tank rocked harder and harder.

"What do they want?" cried Sheena, her voice shrill and trembling.

"They look angry," Dr D whispered.

I stared out at the mermaids, swirling around us like ghosts. They reached out their hands and began clutching at the tank. They smacked their tails on the water. The dark waters tossed and churned.

Suddenly I knew. I knew what they wanted.

"Revenge," I murmured. "They've come for revenge. We took their friend. And now they're going to pay us back."

Shadowy hands pressed against the glass.

"They're pulling us under!" Dr D cried.

I gasped in terror, staring out at the hands, black outlines against the glass.

Then, suddenly, the tank began to rise. Up out of the water, higher and higher.

"Huh? What's happening?" asked Sheena.

"They—they're pushing us back up!" I cried happily.

"The mermaids aren't taking revenge— they're saving us!" Dr D exclaimed.

The tank brushed up against the *Cassandra*. I could see the mermaids' tiny hands working above us.

The clamps popped open. The screen was pulled off.

With a happy groan, Dr D boosted Sheena up. She scrambled on board the boat.

Then I climbed aboard, and we both helped pull Dr D out of the tank.

We were drenched, shivering from the cold. But we were safe.

The mermaids swarmed around the boat, their pale eyes peering up at us.

"Thank you," Dr D called down to them. "Thank you for saving our lives."

I realized this was the second time a mermaid had saved my life. I owed them more than ever now.

"We've got to get the kidnapped mermaid back," I said. "Who knows what Alexander and those creeps will do to her!"

"Yeah," cried Sheena. "Look what they tried to do to us!"

"I wish we could rescue her," Dr D murmured, shaking his head. "But I don't see how we can. How will we find the kidnappers' boat in the dark? They're long gone by now."

But I knew there had to be a way. I leaned over the rail, peering down at the mermaids floating beside us, chattering and cooing in the moonlight.

"Help us!" I pleaded with them. "We want to find your friend. Please—can you take us to her?"

I held my breath and waited. Would the mermaids understand me? Would they be able to help us—somehow?

The mermaids chattered and whistled to one another. Then one of them—a dark-haired mermaid with an extra-long tail—moved to the head of the group.

She began whistling and clicking to the other mermaids. She seemed to be giving orders.

The three of us stared in amazement as the mermaids began to form a long line, one mermaid after the other, stretching far out to sea.

"Do you think they're going to lead us to the kidnappers?" I asked.

"Maybe," Dr D replied thoughtfully. "But how will the mermaids find the boat?" He rubbed his chin. "I know. I'll bet they'll use their sonar. I wish I had time to really listen to those sounds they're making—"

"Look, Dr D!" Sheena interrupted. "The mermaids are swimming away!"

We watched the dark figures slide away through the rolling black waters.

"Quick!" I cried. "We've got to follow them."

"Too dangerous," Dr D replied, sighing. "We can't fight Alexander and four big masked men by ourselves!"

He paced back and forth on the narrow deck. "We should call the island police," he said finally. "But what would we say? That we're chasing after a kidnapped mermaid? No one would believe us."

"Dr D, we have to follow them. Please!" I

pleaded. "The mermaids are swimming out of sight!"

He stared at me for a long moment. "Okay. Let's get going," he said finally.

I hurried to the stern to untie the dinghy. Dr D dropped it into the water and jumped in. Sheena and I followed. Dr D started the motor— and we raced after the shimmering line of mermaids.

The mermaids glided so quickly through the rolling waters, it was hard for the small boat to keep up with them.

About fifteen or twenty minutes later, we found ourselves in a small, deserted cove. The moon drifted out of the clouds. It cast pale light on a dark boat anchored near the shore.

Dr D cut the motor so the kidnappers wouldn't hear us approaching.

"They must be asleep," he whispered.

"How can Alexander sleep after what he did to us?" said Sheena. "He left us to drown!"

"Money can make people do terrible things," Dr D replied sadly. "But it's good they think we're dead. They won't be expecting us."

"But where's the mermaid?" I whispered, staring at the dark boat, bobbing gently under the misty moonlight.

We drifted silently towards the darkened boat.

Well, we've found the kidnappers, I thought, holding on to the side of the dinghy as we drew near.

There's just one problem.

What do we do next?

The air became very still. The kidnappers' boat sat gently on the calm, glassy waters of the cove.

"What happened to all the mermaids?" Sheena whispered.

I shrugged. There was no sign of them. I imagined them swimming way down below the surface, hiding.

Suddenly, at the side of the kidnappers' boat, I saw ripples in the water.

Slowly, silently, our dinghy glided towards the boat. I stared at the ripples, trying to see what was making them. Then I saw a flash of blonde hair in the moonlight.

"The mermaid!" I whispered. "There she is!"

She was floating in the water, tied to the back of the kidnappers' boat.

"They must not have a tank to keep her in," Dr D whispered excitedly. "Lucky for us."

Suddenly, we saw other figures rippling the water. Mermaids arched up, circling the captured mermaid. I saw tail fins raised like giant fans. I saw hands reach around the mermaid, hands tugging at the rope that held her.

The waters tossed quietly as the figures worked.

"The mermaids are setting her free," I whispered.

"What are we going to do?" Sheena asked.

"We'll just make sure she gets away safely," Dr D replied. "Then we'll slip away. The kidnappers will never know we were here."

We watched the mermaids struggle with the rope as our dinghy washed up against the kidnappers' boat.

"Come on, mermaids!" Sheena urged under her breath. "Hurry!"

"Maybe they need some help," I said.

Dr D began to steer toward the mermaids.

I gasped as a light flared on the kidnappers' boat. A match set flame to a torch.

An angry voice boomed, "What do you think you're doing?"

228

I ducked away as the flaming torch was thrust in my face.

Behind the torch, I could see the kidnapper glaring down at me. He had quickly pulled on his black mask. It covered only the top of his face.

I heard a clambering sound, cries of surprise. Alexander and the other three kidnappers appeared on the deck.

"How did you get here?" demanded the man with the torch. "Why aren't you dead?"

"We've come for the mermaid," Dr D called up to him. "You can't keep her here!"

The torch swung past my head. I stood up in the dinghy and took a swipe at it, trying to knock it into the water.

"Billy, no!" cried Dr D.

The kidnapper pulled the torch away. I fell forward in the dinghy, toppling over on Sheena.

"Give us back the mermaid!" Dr D demanded.

"Finders, keepers," the kidnapper muttered. "You've made a long trip for nothing. And now look—your boat is on fire."

He lowered the torch to the dinghy and set it aflame.

The flames flared up, bright orange and yellow against the blue-black sky. They spread quickly across the front of the dinghy.

Sheena uttered a terrified scream and tried to back away from the flames.

In a panic, she started to leap into the water—but Dr D pulled her back. "Don't leave the boat! You'll drown!"

The fire crackled. The bright flames shot higher.

Dr D grabbed a yellow life jacket from the bottom of the dinghy and started frantically beating out the fire.

"Billy—get a life jacket!" he yelled. "Sheena—find the bucket. Throw water on the flames—hurry!"

I found a life jacket and beat at the flames. Sheena dumped seawater on them as fast as she could.

Over the crackling flames, I heard Alexander

shout, "Get the mermaid aboard. Let's get out of here!"

"Dr D!" I cried. "They're getting away!"

Then I heard the kidnappers yelling. "The mermaid! Where's the mermaid?"

I turned to the side of the boat. The mermaid was gone. Her friends had freed her.

One of the kidnappers reached down from his boat and grabbed me. "What did you do with the mermaid?" he demanded.

"Let him go!" shouted Dr D.

I tried to squirm away from the kidnapper. He held me tight. Then I saw another kidnapper swing a club at Dr D's head.

Dr D dodged the club. The kidnapper tried to hit him in the stomach. Dr D dodged again.

I kicked and squirmed. Sheena tugged at the kidnapper's hands, trying to help me escape.

The third kidnapper picked her up by the wrists and threw her to the floor of the dinghy.

"Let go of the kids!" pleaded Dr D. "Alexander! Help us!"

Alexander didn't move from his spot on the deck. He stood with his brawny arms crossed in front of him, calmly watching the fight.

The flames had nearly been quenched, but they suddenly flared up again.

"Sheena—the fire!" I cried. "Put out the fire!"

232

She grabbed the bucket and poured seawater everywhere.

One of the kidnappers kicked the bucket from her hands. It landed in the water with a splash.

Sheena picked up a life jacket and beat the last of the flames out.

"Drop down into their boat and toss them in the water!" I heard a kidnapper shout up above.

A man started to lower himself to our dinghy. But suddenly he lurched forward, his arms flailing. He let out a cry of surprise as his boat began to rock violently to the left. It looked as if it had been slammed by a huge wave.

The kidnappers cried out as their boat began to rock back and forth. Slowly at first. Then violently. Gripping the sides of the dinghy, I watched them clinging to the rail, screaming in confusion and surprise.

Dr D slowly stood up, trying to see what was happening.

The boat tossed violently, as if bucking tall waves.

The mermaids. I could see them now.

They had surrounded the kidnappers' ship and were rocking it hard.

Hard. Harder. The kidnappers hung on helplessly.

"Mission accomplished!" Dr D cried happily. He started up the motor and we roared off.

Turning back, I could see the boat tilting and

rocking in the water. And I could see our mermaid swimming free, behind the other mermaids in the shimmering waves.

"She got away!" I cried. "She's free!"

"I hope she'll be all right," said Sheena.

"We'll look for her tomorrow," said Dr D as he steered us back to the sea lab. "We know where to find her now."

Sheena glanced at me. I glanced back.

Oh, no, I thought. After all this, it can't be true.

Is Dr D going to catch the mermaid again—and give her to the zoo?

Sheena and I met in the galley the next morning. Since Alexander was gone, we had to make our own breakfasts.

"Do you think the mermaid went back to the lagoon?" asked Sheena.

"Probably," I replied. "That's where she lives."

She spooned some cereal into her mouth and chewed with a thoughtful look on her face.

"Sheena," I said, "if someone gave you a million pounds, would you show them where the mermaid lives?"

"No," Sheena replied. "Not if they wanted to capture her."

"Me, neither," I said. "That's what I don't get. Dr D is a great guy. I just can't believe he'd—"

I stopped. I heard a noise. The sound of a motor.

Sheena listened. She heard it, too.

We dropped our spoons and ran up on deck.

Dr D was standing on the deck, staring out to sea.

A boat was approaching. A white boat with MARINA ZOO stencilled on the side in large letters.

"The zoo people!" I said to Sheena. "They're here!"

What would our uncle do? I wondered with growing dread. Would he tell them where the mermaid was? Would he accept the million pounds?

Sheena and I ducked behind the cockpit. We watched the Marina Zoo boat tie up beside the *Cassandra*. I recognized Mr Showalter and Ms Wickman.

Mr Showalter tossed a rope to Dr D. Ms Wickman jumped aboard.

The zoo people smiled and shook Dr D's hand. He nodded at them solemnly.

"We had word from the fishermen on Santa Anita that you've found the mermaid," Mr Showalter said. "We're ready to take her with us now."

Ms Wickman opened her briefcase and pulled out a slender envelope. "Here is a cheque for one million pounds, Dr Deep," she said, smiling.

"We've made it out to you and the *Cassandra Research Lab*."

She held out the cheque to my uncle.

I peered out from behind the cockpit. *Please don't take it, Dr D*, I pleaded silently. *Please don't take the cheque.*

"Thank you very much," my uncle said. He reached out a hand and took the cheque from her.

"A million pounds means a great deal to me and my work," Dr D said. "Your zoo has been very generous. That's why I'm sorry I have to do this."

He raised the envelope and tore it in half.

The two zoo people gasped in surprise.

"I can't take the money," Dr D said.

"Just what are you saying, Dr Deep?" Mr Showalter demanded.

"You sent me on a wild goose chase," my uncle replied. "I have searched these waters thoroughly ever since you left. With my equipment, I have searched every inch of the lagoon and all the surrounding waters. I am now more convinced than ever before that mermaids do not exist."

"Yaaaay!" I screamed to myself. I wanted to jump up and down and cheer my head off—but I stayed hidden with Sheena behind the cockpit.

"But what about the fishermen's stories?" Ms Wickman protested.

"The local fishermen have told mermaid stories for years," Dr D told her. "I think they believe they've really seen mermaids rising through the mist on foggy days. But what they have seen are only fish, or dolphins, or manatees, or even swimmers. Because mermaids don't exist. They're fantasy creatures."

Mr Showalter and Ms Wickman both sighed in disappointment.

"Are you sure about this?" Mr Showalter asked.

"Completely sure," my uncle replied firmly. "My equipment is very sensitive. It can pick up the tiniest minnow."

"We respect your opinion, Dr Deep," Mr Showalter said with some sadness. "You're the leading expert on exotic sea creatures. That's why we came to you in the first place."

"Thank you," said Dr D. "Then I hope you'll take my advice and drop your hunt for a mermaid."

"I guess we'll have to," said Ms Wickman. "Thank you for trying, Dr Deep."

They all shook hands. Then the zoo people got back on their boat and motored away.

The coast was clear. Sheena and I came bursting out of our hiding place.

"Dr D!" cried Sheena, throwing her arms

around him. "You're the greatest!"

A wide grin spread over Dr D's face. "Thanks, guys," he said. "From now on, none of us will say anything to anyone about mermaids. Is it a deal?"

"It's a deal," Sheena instantly agreed.

"Deal," I said. We all shook hands.

The mermaid was our secret.

I swore I'd never mention the mermaid to anyone. But I wanted to see her one last time. I wanted to say goodbye.

After lunch, Sheena and Dr D went to their cabins to nap. We had been up for most of the night, after all. I pretended to take a nap, too.

But once they were asleep, I sneaked out of my cabin and slipped into the bright blue water.

I swam over to the lagoon to search for the mermaid.

The sun was high in a pale blue sky. It glowed down on the still lagoon waters, making them glitter as if covered in gold.

Mermaid? Where are you? I wondered.

I was just past the reef when I felt a playful tug on my leg.

Sheena? I thought. Had she followed me *again*?

I spun around to catch her.

No one there.

Seaweed, probably, I thought. I kept swimming.

A few seconds later, I felt the tug again. Harder this time.

Hey—it must the mermaid! I told myself.

I turned once again to search for her.

The water rippled.

"Mermaid?" I called.

A head popped out of the water.

A gigantic, slimy, dark green head.

With one enormous eye.

And a mouthful of jagged teeth.

"The sea monster!" I shrieked. "The sea monster!"

Would they believe me this time?

Go Eat Worms

Before the worms turned mean, before they slithered out to get their revenge, Todd Barstow had a great time with them.

Todd collected worms. He built a worm farm in his basement.

He studied them. He played with them. He did experiments with them. Sometimes he carried them around with him.

Sometimes he scared people with them. Especially his sister, Regina.

He liked to dangle the long, purple ones in front of Regina's face. Sometimes he dropped them down her back or into her long, brown hair.

He liked to torture Regina's best friend, too. Her name was Beth Baker, and she always screamed a high, squeaky scream whenever Todd surprised her with a big, slimy worm.

"You're disgusting, Todd!" Beth would squeal.

This always made Todd very happy.

Todd's best friend, Danny Fletcher, didn't really understand why Todd was so interested in worms. But Danny *did* understand how much fun it was to surprise people and make them scream. So he spent a lot of time with Todd.

In fact, the two of them were almost always together. They even sat together in Miss Grant's class, where they whispered a lot, planning what to do next with Todd's worms.

Todd didn't look at all mischievous. In fact, he usually had a very serious expression on his face. He had dark brown eyes under short, wavy brown hair. No one ever saw his hair. It was always covered by the silver-and-black Raiders cap he wore day and night.

He was tall and skinny. His mother said he was as skinny as a worm. Todd never thought that was funny. He took worms seriously.

Danny looked more like a joker. He had a round, chubby face under curly red hair, and a really goofy grin. His round blue eyes always lit up when Todd was about to spring a big, wet worm on an unsuspecting victim.

Whenever Todd succeeded in making someone scream in surprise, Danny would toss back his head, let out a high-pitched cheer, and slap Todd hard on the back with his chubby, freckled hand. Then the two of them would screech with laughter, roll around on the floor, and enjoy their victory.

244

They had a great time with worms.

But whenever anyone asked Todd why he collected them, and why he was so interested in them, Todd's expression would turn serious, and he'd say, "Because I want to be a scientist when I grow up."

"How many worms do you have?" someone asked him.

"Not enough," he replied.

He was always digging up more. Looking for champions. He liked them long and purple and kind of fat.

And squishy. Squishy was very important.

Sunday night it had rained. The ground was still wet as Todd and Regina walked to school on Monday morning. Todd knew the worms would all be coming up for air.

He found Danny at the water fountain outside their classroom. Danny had a finger pressed over the fountain spout, and when kids passed by, he made the water squirt all over them.

Todd lowered his Raiders cap over his forehead as he leaned close to Danny. "Meet me behind second base in the playground," he whispered. "As soon as the lunch bell rings."

Danny nodded. He didn't have to ask why. He knew that Todd's favourite place to dig up fresh worms was the bare patch of ground behind second base on the softball diamond.

The ground there was soft and rich. And after a good rain, the two boys could shovel up ten to fifteen worms without even trying.

Todd kept a gardening shovel in his locker, as well as a small metal bucket with a lid. He was always ready to collect worms when the time was right.

In class that morning, everyone was talking about the big Science Expo to be held in the gym on Saturday. Some kids already had their projects done.

Debby Brewster was bragging about how she was going to win the new computer, the grand prize, by making electricity. Someone shouted out, "Go fly a kite!" and everyone laughed. The whole class was tired of Debby's constant bragging.

Todd's project was just about finished. It had worms in it, of course.

It was a worm house. A little house Todd's father had helped him build, about the size of a doll's house. One side was cut away and covered with a pane of glass so you could see in. The house was filled with dirt. And you could see all of the worms—a whole worm family—crawling from room to room.

Danny's project was really boring. He was building the solar system out of balloons.

He wanted to share Todd's project and work

on it with him. But Todd wouldn't let him. "I don't want to share the computer," Todd had said.

"But I helped you dig up the worms!" Danny protested.

"I dug up most of them," Todd replied.

And so Todd forced Danny to do his own project. Danny blew up different-coloured balloons for all the planets and taped them on a big black sheet of card.

Very boring.

"What makes you so sure you're going to win the grand prize?" Danny asked Todd as he hurried to catch up with him in the playground at lunchtime.

"I had a look at the other projects," Todd replied. "My project is the only one with real, living creatures. Except for Heather's snails."

"Heather has done a lot of experiments with her snails," Danny commented.

"So what?" Todd snapped. "Snails are for babies. We had snails in first grade. No one cares about snails in *sixth* grade. No way they can compete with worms."

"I guess you're right," Danny replied, scratching his red hair.

They squatted down as they reached the bare spot behind second base. Todd handed Danny his spare shovel.

The playground was empty. Everyone else was inside eating lunch.

The ground was still soft and wet. Worms were poking their heads up from little puddles. One long worm crawled on top of the dirt.

"The rain makes them all come up," said Todd, beginning to dig. "This is excellent!"

He didn't know what kind of trouble was waiting under the ground.

"Look out. You cut that one in two," Todd warned.

Danny grinned. "So what? Now you've got two little ones."

"But I only like big ones," Todd replied, carefully sliding his shovel under a long, fat worm.

"How many more do you need? My stomach is growling," Danny complained, glancing back at the long, redbrick school building.

"Just a few more," Todd said, lowering the fat worm into the bucket. "He's a squirmer, isn't he?"

Danny groaned. "Everyone else is eating lunch, and I'm out here digging in the mud."

"It's for science," Todd said seriously.

"This one is as big as a snake. Did you ever think of collecting snakes?" Danny asked.

"No," Todd replied quickly, digging deep into the mud. "No way."

"Why not?"

"Because I like worms," Todd said.

"What's the *real* reason?" Danny demanded.

"My parents won't let me," Todd muttered.

The two boys continued to dig for another few minutes until the ground started to rumble. Danny dropped his shovel.

"What's that?" he asked.

"Huh?" Todd didn't seem to notice.

The ground rumbled a little harder. This time everything shook.

Todd pitched forward, dropping on to his hands and knees. He gazed up at Danny, surprised. "Hey—don't push me."

"I didn't!" Danny protested.

"Then what—?" Todd started. But the ground shook again. And the dirt made a soft cracking sound.

"I—I don't like this!" Danny stammered.

Without another word, both boys started to run.

But the ground trembled again, and the cracking sound beneath their trainers grew louder. Closer.

"Earthquake!" Todd screamed. "Earthquake!"

Todd and Danny sprinted across the field and the playground and burst into the lunchroom.

Both boys had red faces. Both of them were breathing hard.

"Earthquake!" Todd shouted. "It's an earthquake!"

Chairs scraped. Conversations stopped. Everyone turned to stare at the two of them.

"Duck under the tables!" Danny screamed shrilly. "Quick, everyone! The ground is shaking!"

"Earthquake! Earthquake!"

Everyone just laughed.

No one moved.

No one wanted to fall for a stupid practical joke.

Todd spotted Beth and Regina across the lunchroom at the window. He and Danny darted over to them.

"Get away from the window!" Todd warned.

251

"The ground is cracking apart!" Danny cried.

Regina's mouth dropped open. She didn't know whether to believe them or not. Regina, the worrier, was always ready to believe a disaster waited just around the corner.

But all the other kids in the huge lunchroom were laughing their heads off.

"We don't get earthquakes in Ohio," Beth said simply, making a disgusted face at Todd.

"But—but—but—" Todd sputtered.

"Didn't you feel it?" Danny demanded breathlessly, his round, chubby face still bright red. "Didn't you feel the ground shake?"

"We didn't feel anything," Beth replied.

"Didn't you *hear* it?" Todd cried. "I—I was so freaked, I dropped all my worms." He sank into the chair next to his sister.

"No one believes you. It's a stupid joke, Todd," Regina told him. "Better luck next time."

"But—but—"

Regina turned away from her sputtering brother and started talking to Beth again. "As I was saying, his head is way too big for his body."

"He looks okay to me," Beth replied.

"No. We'll have to cut his head off," Regina insisted, frowning into her bowl of noodle soup.

"Major surgery?" Beth asked. "Are you sure? If we cut his head off, it'll show. It really will."

"But if his head is too big, what choice do we have?" Regina whined.

"Huh? What are you talking about?" Todd demanded. "What about the earthquake?"

"Todd, we're talking about our science fair project," Beth said impatiently.

"Yeah. Go out and play in the earthquake!" Regina snapped. "We've got problems with Christopher Robin."

Todd sniggered. "What a stupid name for a bird."

Regina stuck out her tongue at him and then turned her back. She and Beth began discussing their project again.

They both agreed they probably should have tried something a little easier. And smaller.

They were building an enormous robin out of papier-mâché. It was supposed to be lifelike in every detail, except size.

But the girls quickly discovered that papier-mâché isn't the most lifelike material around. It was hard to get the wings to stick to the body. It was even harder to get the huge round body to stand on the spindly wooden legs.

And now Regina was convinced that the bird's head was much too big for its body.

They had used an entire quart of orange paint on the bird's chest. Now, if they had to cut the head off and make a new one, the paint job would be ruined!

"Maybe we could just shave a little off the top," Beth suggested, taking the last crisp from her bag and crinkling the bag between her hands. "Can I have some of your soup?"

"You can finish it," Regina replied, sliding the bowl across the table. "I'm not very hungry."

"There's going to be an aftershock," Todd warned, staring out of the window.

"Yeah. There's always an aftershock after an earthquake," Danny agreed.

"I can't believe you're sitting here calmly, talking about your stupid project," Todd said.

"It's not a stupid project!" Beth replied angrily.

"Todd, go eat worms!" Regina exclaimed. It was her favourite thing to say to her brother. She said it at least ten times a day.

"Beth is already eating worms," Todd said, gazing down at the bowl of soup.

Danny laughed.

"Give me a break, Todd," Beth muttered, rolling her eyes.

"No. Really," Todd insisted. "What kind of soup is that?"

"Chicken noodle," Beth replied warily. She took a spoonful, slurping the soup off the spoon.

"Well, there's a worm in your soup," Todd said with a serious face.

"Todd, you're not funny," Beth replied. "Give up."

"Want to bet?" Todd challenged.

"Bet? What do you mean 'bet'?" Beth said.

"I'll bet you a dollar there's a worm in your soup," Todd told her, his dark eyes lighting up.

Danny leaned across the table, a wide grin frozen on his chubby face. "Yummm," he said, licking his lips. "A big fat purple one! Can I have a taste?"

"You two are pathetic," Regina muttered.

"Bet a dollar?" Todd challenged, ignoring his sister.

"Sure. It's a bet," Beth said.

She reached across the table and shook Todd's hand to seal the bet. Then she ran the soup spoon through the bowl several times to show him there was no worm.

Todd reached under the table. Then a smile crossed his face as he brought his hand up—and dropped a fat purple worm into Beth's soup.

The worm wriggled and squirmed as it hit the hot soup.

"Oooh, yuk!" Beth screamed.

Danny let out a loud laugh and slapped Todd gleefully on the back, nearly knocking Todd off the chair.

"Pay up, Beth," Todd demanded. "You lost the bet."

"You guys are sick," Regina murmured, making a disgusted face, forcing herself not to look into the soup bowl.

"Yuck! Disgusting!" Beth was shrieking.

The worm slipped and swam through the noodles.

"You said you dropped your worms outside," Regina accused angrily.

Todd shrugged, a big grin on his face. "I lied!"

Danny laughed even harder. He pounded the table gleefully with his fists, making the soup bowl bounce up and down.

"Hey!" Suddenly Todd's smile faded. He stared out of the lunchroom window at the playground.

"Look!" He hit Danny's shoulder, then pointed out towards second base, to the bare spot behind the base. "What's going on out there?" he cried.

Todd walked over to the window and peered out, pressing his nose against the glass. "What is Patrick MacKay doing in my worm-digging spot?" he demanded angrily.

Danny stepped beside Todd. He squinted out into the grey afternoon. "Are you sure that's Patrick MacKay?"

The sky darkened as the low clouds gathered. The boy on the playground was half covered by shadow. But Todd recognized him anyway.

That snobby, stuck-up, rich kid. Patrick MacKay.

He was bent over the bare spot of mud behind second base, working feverishly.

"What is he *doing* out there?" Todd repeated. "That's my best worm spot!"

"He's digging up worms, too!" Regina declared from the table.

"Huh?" Todd spun round to find his sister smirking at him.

"Patrick is digging up worms for the Science Expo," she told him, unable to hide her joy. "He's doing a worm project, too."

"But he *can't!*" Todd sputtered in a high, shrill voice.

"Whoa! What a copycat!" Danny declared.

"He can't do a worm project! *I'm* doing the worm project!" Todd insisted, turning back to stare at Patrick through the glass.

"It's a free country," Regina replied smugly. She and Beth laughed. They were enjoying seeing Todd squirm for a change.

"But he's not into worms!" Todd continued, very upset. "He doesn't collect worms! He doesn't study worms! He's just copying me!"

"Look at him, digging in your spot," Danny murmured, shaking his head bitterly.

"Patrick is a nice guy," Beth remarked. "He doesn't act like an idiot and put worms in people's soup."

"He's an idiot," Todd insisted angrily, staring hard out of the window. "He's a total idiot."

"He's a copycat idiot," Danny added.

"His worm project is going to be better than yours," Regina teased him.

Todd's dark eyes burned into his sister's. "You know what it is? You know what Patrick's project is?"

Regina had a smug smile on her lips. She tossed back her brown hair. Then she made a zipper sign, moving her fingers across her lips.

"I'll never tell," she said.

"What is it?" Todd demanded. "Tell me."

Regina shook her head.

"Tell me, Beth," Todd insisted, narrowing his eyes menacingly at her.

"No way," Beth replied, glancing merrily at Regina.

"Then I'll ask him myself," Todd declared. "Come on, Danny."

The two boys started running through the lunchroom. They were nearly at the door when Todd ran into their teacher.

Miss Grant was carrying her lunch tray high over her head, stepping round a group of kids in the aisle. Todd just didn't see her.

He bumped her from behind.

She uttered a cry of surprise—and her tray flew out of her hands. The tray and the plates clattered loudly on to the floor. And her food— salad and a bowl of spaghetti—dropped around her feet.

"What is your hurry, young man?" she snapped at Todd.

"Uh . . . sorry," Todd murmured. It was the only reply he could think of.

Miss Grant bent to examine her brown shoes, which were now orange, covered with wet clumps of spaghetti.

"It was an accident," Todd said impatiently,

259

fiddling with his Raiders cap.

"It certainly was," the teacher replied coldly. "Perhaps I should speak to you after school about why we don't run in the lunchroom?"

"Perhaps," Todd agreed. Then he bolted past her, running through the door faster than he had ever run.

"Well done, Todd!" Danny exclaimed, running beside him.

"It wasn't my fault," Todd told him. "She stepped in front of me."

"The bell is going to ring," Danny warned as they made their way out of the back door.

"I don't care," Todd replied breathlessly. "I've got to find out what that copycat is doing with worms!"

Patrick was still bent over the mud behind second base. He was scooping up worms with a silvery towel that looked brand-new, then dropping them into a metal bait can.

He was a slim, good-looking boy with wavy blond hair and blue eyes. He had started school in September. His family had moved to Ohio from Pasadena. He was always telling everyone how California was so much better.

He didn't brag about how rich he was. But he wore designer jeans, and his mother brought him to school every morning in a long, white Lincoln. So Todd and the others at William

Tecumseh Sherman Middle School worked it out.

Patrick was in Regina's class. A few weeks after school started, he'd had a big birthday party and invited everyone in his class. Including Regina.

She reported that Patrick had a whole funfair, with rides and everything, in his back garden. Todd pretended he didn't care that he wasn't invited.

The sky grew even darker as Danny and Todd stood over Patrick in the playground. "What are you doing, Patrick?" Todd demanded.

"Digging," Patrick replied, glancing up from his work.

"Digging up worms?" Todd asked, his hands pressed against the waist of his jeans.

Patrick nodded. He started digging again. He pulled up a long, dark brown one that Todd would have loved to own.

"*I'm* doing a worm project," Todd told him.

"I know," Patrick replied, concentrating on his work. "Me, too."

"What is it?" Danny chimed in. "What's your project, Patrick?"

Patrick didn't reply. He dug up a tiny, pale worm, examined it, and tossed it back.

"What's your project? Tell us," Todd demanded.

"You really want to know?" Patrick asked,

raising his blue eyes to them. The wind ruffled his blond hair, but the hair immediately fell back into place.

Todd felt a raindrop on his shoulder. Then one on the top of his head.

"What's your project?" Todd repeated.

"Okay, okay," Patrick said, wiping dirt off his hands. "I'll tell you. My project is . . ."

The class bell rang. The sharp clang cut through the rising wind. The rain started to patter loudly against the ground.

"We've got to go in," Danny urged, tugging at Todd's sleeve.

"Wait," Todd said, his eyes on Patrick. "Tell me now!" he insisted.

"But we'll be late!" Danny insisted, tugging at Todd again. "And we're getting soaked."

Patrick climbed to his feet. "I think I've got all the worms I need." He shook wet dirt off the silvery towel.

"So what is your worm project?" Todd repeated, ignoring the pattering rain and Danny's urgent requests to get back inside the school.

Patrick grinned at him, revealing about three hundred perfect, white teeth. "I'm teaching them to fly," he said.

"Huh?"

"I'm putting cardboard wings on them and

teaching them to fly. Wait till you see it! It's a riot!" He burst out laughing.

Danny leaned close to Todd. "Is he for real?" he whispered.

"Of course not!" Todd shot back. "Don't be an idiot, Danny. He's having us on."

"Hey—you're not funny," Danny told Patrick angrily.

"We're late, guys. Let's get going," Patrick said, his grin fading. He started towards the school building.

But Todd moved quickly to block his path. "Tell me the truth, Patrick. What are you planning to do?"

Patrick started to reply.

But a low rumbling sound made him stop.

They all heard it. A muffled roar that made the ground shake.

The worm can fell out of Patrick's hand. His blue eyes opened wide in surprise—and fear.

The rumbling gave way to a loud, cracking noise. It sounded as if the whole playground were splitting apart.

"Wh-what's *happening*?" Patrick stammered.

"Run!" Todd screamed as the ground trembled and shook. "Run for your life!"

264

"Why are you so late? Where've you been? In another earthquake?" Regina teased.

"Ha-ha," Todd said bitterly. "Danny and I weren't making it up. It happened again! And Patrick was there, too."

"How come no one else felt it?" Regina demanded. "I had the radio on after school. And there was nothing about an earthquake on the news."

It was nearly five o'clock. Todd had found his sister in the garage, up on an aluminium ladder, working hard on her giant robin. Somehow she had managed to get clumps of papier-mâché in her hair and down the front of her T-shirt.

"I don't want to talk about the earthquake," Todd muttered, stepping into the garage. "I know I'm right."

The rain had ended just before school finished. But the driveway was still puddled with water.

His wet trainers squeaked as he made his way to Regina's ladder.

"Where's Beth?" he asked.

"She had to go and get her brace tightened," Regina told him, concentrating on smoothing out the papier-mâché beak. She let out a loud groan. "I can't get this beak smooth."

Todd kicked dejectedly at an old tyre that was leaning against the garage wall.

"Look out!" Regina called.

A wet clump of papier-mâché landed at Todd's feet with a plop. "You missed me!" he cried, ducking away.

"So? Where've you been?" Regina asked.

"Miss Grant kept me after school. She gave me a long lecture."

"About what?" Regina stopped to examine her work.

"I don't know. Something about running in school," Todd replied. "How are you going to get this stupid bird to the science fair?"

"Carry it," Regina answered without hesitating. "It's big, but it's really light. I don't suppose you would help Beth and me?"

"I don't suppose I would," Todd told her, wrapping his hand around the broomstick that formed one bird leg.

"Hey—get your paws off!" Regina cried. "Leave it alone!"

Todd obediently backed away.

266

"You're just jealous because Christopher Robin is going to win the computer," Regina said.

"Listen, Reggie—you've *got* to tell me what Patrick MacKay is doing for his worm project," Todd pleaded. "You've *got* to."

She climbed down off the ladder. She saw the big worm in Todd's hand. "What's that for?" she demanded.

"Nothing." Todd's cheeks turned pink.

"You planned to drop that down my back, didn't you?" Regina accused him.

"No. I was just taking it for a walk," Todd told her. He laughed.

"You're a creep," Regina said, shaking her head. "Don't you ever get tired of those stupid worms?"

"No," Todd replied. "So tell me. What's Patrick's project?"

"You want to hear the truth?" Regina asked.

"Yeah."

"The truth is, I don't know," his sister confessed. "I really don't know *what* he's doing."

Todd stared hard at her for a long moment. "You really don't?"

She crossed her heart. "I really don't know."

Todd suddenly had an idea. "Where does he live?" he asked eagerly.

267

The question caught Regina by surprise. "Why?"

"Danny and I can go over there tonight," Todd said. "And I'll ask him what he's doing."

"You're going to go to his house?" Regina asked.

"I've *got* to find out!" Todd exclaimed. "I've worked so hard on my worm house, Reggie. I don't want Patrick the Copycat to do something better."

Regina eyed her brother thoughtfully. "And what will you do for *me* if I tell you where he lives?"

A grin spread over Todd's face. He held up the worm. "If you tell me, I won't put this down your back."

"Ha-ha," Regina replied, rolling her eyes. "You're a real pal, Todd."

"Tell me!" he insisted eagerly, grabbing her by the shoulders.

"Okay, okay. Don't have a cow. Patrick lives on Glen Cove," Regina replied. "I think the number is 100. It's a huge, old mansion. Behind a tall fence."

"Thanks!" Todd said. "Thanks a lot!"

Then, as Regina bent down to pick up the globs of papier-mâché from the garage floor, he dropped the worm down the back of her T-shirt.

"I can't believe we're doing this," Danny complained. "My parents said I couldn't come over. As soon as they went shopping, I ducked out. But if they catch me . . ." His voice trailed off.

"We'll be back home in fifteen minutes," Todd said. He changed gear and pedalled the bike harder. Danny's old bike splashed through a deep puddle at the kerb.

The rain clouds had rolled away. But the wind still gusted, cool and damp. The sun had set about an hour before. Now a thin sliver of moon hung low in the evening sky.

"Where is the house? On Glen Cove?" Danny asked, out of breath.

Todd nodded. He changed gear again. He liked changing back and forth. It was a new bike, and he still hadn't got used to so many gears.

A car rolled towards them rapidly, the glare of its white headlights forcing them to shield their eyes. Danny's bike rolled up on to the kerb, and he nearly toppled over. "Why'd they have their full beam on?" he griped.

"Beats me," Todd replied.

They turned sharply on to Glen Cove. It was a wide street of old houses set back on broad, sloping lawns. The houses were set far apart, separated by dark wooded areas.

"No streetlights," Danny commented. "You'd think rich people could afford streetlights."

"Maybe they like it dark," Todd replied thoughtfully. "You know. It helps keep people away."

"It's a bit creepy here," Danny said softly, leaning over his handlebars.

"Don't be a wimp. Look for 100," Todd said sharply. "That's Patrick's address."

"Wow. Check out that house!" Danny said, slowing down and pointing. "It looks like a castle!"

"I think 100 must be on the next block," Todd called, eagerly pedalling ahead.

"What are we going to say to Patrick?" Danny asked, breathing hard, struggling to catch up.

"I'm just going to ask him if we can see his worm project," Todd replied, his eyes searching the darkness for address signs. "Maybe I'll act like I want to help him out. You know. Give him a few tips on how to take care of the worms."

270

"Nice of you," Danny teased. He chuckled to himself. "What if Patrick says no?"

Todd didn't reply. He hadn't thought of that.

He squeezed the hand brake. "Look." He pointed to an enormous house behind a tall iron fence. "That's his house."

Danny's brakes squealed as he brought his bike to a stop. He lowered his feet to the wet pavement. "Wow."

The house rose up over the broad, tree-filled lawn, black against the purple night sky. It was completely dark. Not a light on anywhere.

"No one at home," Danny said, whispering.

"Good," Todd replied. "This is even better. Maybe we can look down through the basement window or find the window to Patrick's room, and see what he's working on."

"Maybe," Danny replied reluctantly.

Todd glanced around. Patrick's house was the only one on the block. And it was surrounded by woods.

Both boys climbed off their bikes and started to walk them to the driveway.

"I can't believe Patrick would live in such a wreck of a place," Todd said, pulling off his cap and scratching his hair. "I mean, this house is a real dump."

"Maybe his parents are weird or something," Danny suggested as they parked their bikes.

"Maybe," Todd replied thoughtfully.

271

"Sometimes rich people get a little weird," Danny said, climbing on to the porch and ringing the doorbell.

"How would *you* know?" Todd said, sniggering. He pulled his cap back down over his dark hair and rang the bell again. "No answer. Let's check out the back," he said, hopping off the porch.

"What for?" Danny demanded.

"Let's just look in the windows," Todd urged, moving along to the side of the house. "Let's see if we can see anything at all."

As they turned the corner, it grew even darker. The pale sliver of moonlight was reflected in one of the upstairs windows. The only light.

"This is stupid," Danny complained. "It's too dark to see anything inside the house. And, besides—"

He stopped.

"*Now* what's wrong?" Todd demanded impatiently.

"Didn't you hear it? I heard it again," Danny said. "Like a growl. Some kind of animal growl."

Todd didn't hear the growl.

But he saw something enormous running towards them.

He saw the evil red glow of its eyes—unblinking eyes trained on him.

And he knew it was too late to escape.

"Run!" Danny screamed.

But Todd couldn't move.

As the enormous red-eyed monster bounded towards them, Todd pressed his back against a side door.

He nearly fell as the door swung in.

The creature uttered an ugly, threatening growl. Its huge paws thundered over the ground.

"Inside!" Todd screamed. "Danny—get in the house!"

His heart pounding as loudly as the monster's paws, Todd scrambled into the dark house. Danny lurched in behind him, uttering low gasps.

Todd slammed the door shut as the creature attacked.

Its paws struck the windowpane in the door, making the entire door rattle.

"It's a dog!" Todd cried in a choked whisper. "A huge, angry dog!"

273

The dog let out another ferocious growl and leaped at the door. Its paws scraped over the window.

"A dog?" Danny exclaimed shrilly. "I thought it was a *gorilla!*"

The two boys pressed their shoulders against the door, holding it shut. They peered out warily at the big creature.

The dog had sat back on its haunches. It stared in at them, its red eyes glowing. It was panting loudly, its enormous tongue hanging out of its mouth.

"Someone should put that dog on a diet!" Danny exclaimed.

"We could ride him to school!" Todd added.

"How do we get out of here?" Danny asked, turning away from the dog. His eyes searched the dark room.

"He'll go away," Todd said. He swallowed hard. "Probably."

"This place is a dump," Danny said, stepping into the room.

Todd turned to follow Danny. They were in the kitchen, he saw. Pale moonlight floated in through the window. Even in this dim light, Todd could see that something was terribly wrong.

The kitchen counters were bare and covered in dust. There were no appliances—no toaster, no microwave, no refrigerator. There were no dishes or pots and pans in view. Glancing down, Todd saw that the sink was caked with thick dirt.

"Weird," Danny muttered.

The two boys made their way through a short hallway to the dining room.

"Where's the furniture?" Danny asked, gazing in all directions.

The room was empty.

"Maybe they're redecorating or something," Todd guessed.

"This doesn't make sense. Patrick's family is rich," Danny said, shaking his head. "You know how neat Patrick is. He gets upset if his shirt comes untucked."

"I don't get it," Todd replied. "Where do you think he has his worm project?"

The two boys made their way towards the living room. Their trainers scraped over the dusty, bare floor.

"Something is weird here," Danny murmured. "Something is very weird."

They both gasped as they stepped into the living room—and saw the figure hunched at the window.

Saw the decayed green flesh of his face.

Saw the bones of his jaw, open in a hideous toothless grin.

Saw his evil, sunken eyes staring across the room at them.

The heavy silence was broken by the shrill screams of the two boys.

"Go! Go!" Todd cried. He shoved Danny towards the door and stumbled along behind him, keeping his hands on Danny's shoulders.

"Go! Go! Go!"

Through the bare dining room. Across the dust-covered kitchen.

"Go! Go!"

Todd grabbed the doorknob, pulled open the door, and they both burst out of the house.

Had the dog left?

Yes!

"Let's *move!*" Todd cried.

But Danny needed no encouragement. He was already halfway down the driveway, his chubby legs pumping hard, his hands stretched out in front of him as if trying to *pull* himself to safety.

Out of the gate. On to their bikes.

They pedalled furiously. Faster. Faster. Until

their legs ached and they could barely breathe.

And they never looked back.

Who was that hideous, decayed figure in Patrick's house?

And why was the house so dusty, so totally bare?

Todd spent most of the night lying awake in his bed, thinking about it.

But the mystery wasn't cleared up until the next morning.

Yawning sleepily, Todd pulled on the same clothes he had worn the day before. Then he made his way down the hall to go to breakfast.

He stopped outside Regina's bedroom door when he heard her laughing. At first, he thought she was talking to herself.

But then he realized that Regina was on the phone.

So early?

He pressed his ear to the door and listened.

"Isn't it a riot, Beth?" Regina was saying. "I sent them to the wrong address." Regina laughed again. Gleeful laughter.

Todd suddenly snapped wide awake. He pressed his ear tighter against the bedroom door.

"Todd was so desperate, I couldn't resist," Regina was saying. "Know where I sent them?"

There was a short pause. Todd realized he was

holding his breath. He let it out silently and took another one, listening hard.

"I sent them to the old Fosgate mansion," Regina told Beth. She laughed. "Yeah. Right. That old deserted mansion where those kids had that Halloween party. Yeah. You know. They left that dummy with the weird mask in the window."

Another pause.

Todd gritted his teeth as he listened to his sister's triumphant laughter. He could feel every muscle in his body tightening in anger.

"I don't know, Beth. I haven't talked to him yet," Regina was saying. "I heard Todd come in last night. He ran straight to his room and shut the door. He was probably too scared to talk!"

More laughter.

Clenching and unclenching his fists, Todd stepped away from his sister's door. He stopped at the stairs, feeling his face grow red-hot. He was thinking hard.

So Reggie played a little joke on Danny and me, he thought bitterly. So she gave me the wrong address and sent us to that old haunted house.

Ha-ha. Good joke.

Todd felt so angry, he wanted to scream.

Now Regina will be laughing at me about this for ever, he realized. She will make fun of me for the rest of my life.

Her bedroom door opened, and Regina stepped out into the hall. She was pulling her brown hair back into a ponytail.

She stopped when she saw Todd at the top of the stairs. "So, how did it go last night?" she asked him, grinning.

"Fine," he replied casually. He gave her an innocent, wide-eyed stare.

Her grin faded. "Did you go to Patrick's house? Did you talk to him about his worm project?" she demanded, staring back at him, studying his face.

Todd shook his head. "No. Danny and I decided to skip it. We just stayed at Danny's," he lied.

Her dark eyes seemed to dim. She bit her lower lip. Todd could see how disappointed she was.

He turned and made his way down the stairs, feeling a little better.

You want to play jokes, Reggie? he thought.

Okay. Fine.

But now it's *my* turn. My turn to play a mean joke.

Todd smiled. He had already thought of a really good one.

Todd hoisted the cardboard box in both hands. His worm house was packed carefully inside. It was heavier than he thought.

"Where shall I put it?" he asked Mrs Sanger, struggling to keep the heavy box from slipping out of his hands.

"What? I can't hear you!" The science teacher held a clipboard in one hand. She cupped her other hand around her mouth as a megaphone.

It was deafening in the gym as the kids all hurried to set up their science projects in time for the expo. Excited voices competed with scraping chairs and tables, the rattle of boxes being unpacked, and projects of all shapes and sizes being assembled and set up.

"What a crowd!" Todd exclaimed.

"I can't hear you!" Mrs Sanger shouted. She pointed to a long table against the wall. "I think your project goes there, Todd."

Todd started to say something. But he was

interrupted by the crash of shattering glass and a girl's loud scream.

"Was that the *acid*?" Mrs Sanger shouted, her eyes going wide with horror. "Was that the acid?" She pushed past Todd and went tearing across the gym, holding her clipboard in front of her like a shield.

Todd watched a lot of kids gathering around the spot of the accident. Mrs Sanger burst into the circle, and everyone began talking at once.

Around the vast gym, others ignored the excitement and continued feverishly setting up their projects.

The benches had been put out. Some parents and other kids from the school were already seated, waiting to watch the expo and the judging of projects.

Groaning, Todd started to make his way through the crowded gym carrying the cardboard box. He had to stop and chuckle when he caught a glimpse of Regina and Beth.

They had their enormous robin set up close to the benches. The head was the right size now. They had managed to shave it down smoothly.

But some of the tail feathers had got mashed. And they were working frantically to smooth them out.

What losers, Todd thought, grinning.

There's no way they're going to win the computer.

Turning away, he glimpsed Danny's balloon solar system hanging on the back wall. One of the balloons—the one closest to the sun—had already deflated.

Pitiful, Todd thought, shaking his head. That's just pitiful.

He sighed. Poor Danny. I guess I should have let him share my project.

Todd lowered the box on to the table reserved for him.

"Ten minutes, everyone! Ten minutes!" Mrs Sanger was shouting.

No problem, Todd thought.

He opened the box and carefully lifted out the worm house. What a beauty! he thought proudly.

It looked like a perfect little house. Todd had polished the wood frame until it glowed. And he had cleaned the glass until it was spotless.

He put the worm house down carefully on the table and turned it so that the glass side faced the audience on the benches. He gazed into it. He could see the long brown and purple worms crawling from room to room.

He had packed the dirt in carefully. Then he had dropped in more than twenty worms before sealing it all up.

It's a real big family! he thought, grinning.

Once the worm house was in place, Todd pulled out the sign he had made for it and placed the sign beside it on the table.

He stepped back to admire his work. But someone pushed him gently aside.

"Make room. Make room, Todd." It was Mrs Sanger. And to Todd's surprise, she was helping Patrick MacKay carry a long cardboard box to the table.

"Move your project to the side, Todd," the teacher instructed. "You have to share the table."

"Huh? Share?" Todd hesitated.

"Hurry—please!" Mrs Sanger pleaded. "Patrick's box is heavy."

"I'm sharing the table with Patrick?" Todd couldn't hide his unhappiness.

Obediently, he slid his worm house to one side of the table. Then he stood behind the table, watching as Patrick and the teacher unloaded the long box. It was nearly two metres long.

"Is that all *one* worm?" Todd joked.

"Very funny," Patrick muttered. He was straining hard to lift his project on to the table.

"This will be our worm table," Mrs Sanger said, grabbing the end of the box and tugging. Patrick pulled, too.

Todd gasped as Patrick hoisted his project on to the tabletop.

"Very impressive, Patrick," Mrs Sanger commented, straightening her skirt. She hurried off to help someone else.

Todd gaped at the project. It towered over his. It was nearly two metres tall, taller than Patrick!

"Oh, nooooo," Todd moaned to himself. He turned to Patrick. "It—it isn't . . . it *can't* be—!" He choked on the words.

Patrick was busily setting up his sign. He stepped back, checking it out, making sure it was straight.

"Yes, it is!" he said, beaming at Todd. "It's a worm skyscraper!"

"Wow." Todd didn't want to show how upset he was. But he couldn't help it. His legs were trembling. His mouth dropped open. And he started to stutter. "But—but—but—"

I don't believe this! Todd thought miserably.

I built a crummy little worm house. And Patrick made a skyscraper!

It's not fair! *Not fair!*

Patrick doesn't even *like* worms!

He stared at the giant wood-and-glass structure. He could see dozens and dozens of worms inside. They were crawling from floor to floor. There was even a wooden lift with several worms tucked inside.

"Todd—are you okay?" Patrick asked.

"Yeah. Uh . . . fine," Todd replied, trying to force his legs to stop quivering.

"You look a little weird," Patrick said, staring at Todd with his bright blue eyes.

"Uh . . . that's a nice project, Patrick," Todd admitted through clenched teeth. "You could win the big prize."

"You think so?" Patrick replied, as if the thought had never occurred to him. "Thanks, Todd. I got the idea from you. About worms, I mean."

You *stole* the idea, you thief! Todd thought angrily.

I have only one wish for you, Patrick. *Go eat worms!*

"Wow! What's *that*?" Danny's voice broke into Todd's ugly thoughts. He was staring in amazement at Patrick's project.

"It's a worm skyscraper," Patrick told him, beaming with pride.

Danny admired it for a while. Then he turned to Todd. "Why didn't *you* think of that?" he whispered.

Todd gave Danny a hard shove. "Go blow up a balloon," he muttered.

Danny spun around angrily. "Don't shove me—"

Mrs Sanger's voice over the loudspeaker rose over the noise of the gym. "Places by your projects, everyone. The expo is starting. The judges will begin their rounds."

Danny hurried back to his balloon solar system against the wall. Todd watched him make his way past a display of rocks. Danny

285

was swinging his arms as he walked, and he nearly knocked over all the rocks.

Then Todd stepped behind the table. He brushed a speck of dust off the roof of his worm house.

I should just toss it in the trash, he thought miserably. He glanced at Patrick, who stood beside him, grinning from ear to ear, his hands resting on the sides of his magnificent skyscraper.

The copycat is going to win, Todd thought sadly.

He sighed. Only one thing would cheer him up a little. One thing. And gazing across the gym, Todd saw that it was time for it to happen.

The three judges—all teachers from another school—were stepping up to check out Christopher Robin. As they bent low to examine the papier-mâché bird's feet, Todd made his way quickly over to his sister's project.

He wanted a good view.

One judge, a plump young woman in a bright yellow top, examined the tail feathers. Another judge, a man with a shiny bald head, was questioning Regina and Beth. The third judge had her back to Todd. She was running her hand over the bird's swelling orange breast.

Reggie and Beth look really nervous, Todd thought, edging past a display on how trash gets recycled.

Well, they *should* be nervous. What a stupid project.

Todd stopped a few metres in front of the benches. There was a really big audience for the expo, he noticed. The benches were at least two-thirds filled. Mostly parents and younger brothers and sisters of the contestants.

The bald judge kept making notes on a small pad as he questioned Regina and Beth. The other two judges were staring up at the giant robin's beak.

Todd edged closer.

"What's this string?" the judge in the yellow top asked Beth.

"Huh? String?" Beth reacted with surprise. She and Regina raised their eyes to the yellow beak.

"What string?" Regina demanded.

Too late.

The judge in the yellow top pulled the string.

The beak lowered, revealing a surprise inside.

"Ohhhh."

"Yuck!"

Disgusted groans rose up from the audience. And Regina and Beth started to scream.

Fat worms wriggled out from inside the bird's beak.

Some of them wriggled out and rained down on the judges.

A huge purple worm plopped on to the bald judge's head. The angry judge's red face darkened until it nearly matched the purple worm.

Early that morning, Todd had packed about thirty worms in there. He was glad to see that most of them had stayed in the beak.

People on the benches were groaning and moaning. "That's *sick!*" someone yelled.

"Disgusting! That's so disgusting!" a little boy kept repeating.

The judges were demanding to know if Regina and Beth had stuffed the worms up there as a joke.

Mrs Sanger was glaring angrily at them. The two girls were sputtering their apologies.

It was a thrilling moment, Todd thought. A thrilling moment.

About ten or fifteen worms were wriggling across the gym floor. Todd started to edge back to his table.

"There he is! My brother!" he heard Regina shout. He glanced up to see her pointing furiously at him. "Todd did it! It had to be Todd!"

He gave her an innocent shrug. "I thought Christopher Robin looked hungry—so I fed him!" he called. Then he hurried back to his worm house.

A big grin on his handsome face, Patrick slapped Todd a high five. "Good stuff!"

Todd grudgingly accepted the congratulations. He didn't want to be friends with Patrick. He wanted Patrick to go eat worms.

He glanced back at Danny. Danny was frantically blowing up a balloon. The rings had fallen off Saturn. And someone had accidentally popped Pluto.

Todd smiled. He felt pretty good. His little joke had worked perfectly. Revenge was sweet. He had paid Regina back for sending him to that creepy old house.

But his smile faded as he glanced at Patrick's skyscraper and remembered that he was going to miss out on the grand prize.

It took the school janitor a few minutes to

round up all the worms. The crowd on the benches cheered him on as he scooped up the wiggling worms one by one and dropped them into an empty coffee jar.

After that, the expo continued calmly and quietly. The judges moved from project to project, asking questions, making notes.

Todd took a deep breath when they approached his table. Don't get excited, he warned himself. The worm house looks really puny next to the worm skyscraper.

He had a sudden urge to bump the table, to shake it really hard. Maybe the skyscraper would topple over, and the house would be left standing.

I could pretend it was just an accident, Todd thought.

Evil thoughts.

But he didn't do it.

The three judges spent about ten seconds looking at Todd's project. They didn't ask Todd a single question.

Then they gazed at Patrick's skyscraper for at least five minutes. "How did you get all those worms in there?" the bald judge asked.

"I love the elevator!"

"How many worms are there in total?"

"Can worms survive in a *real* skyscraper?"

"And what does this project prove about gravity?"

Yak yak yak, Todd thought bitterly.

He watched the judges coo and carry on over Patrick's project. He wanted to grab all three of them and say, "He's a copycat! I'm the real worm guy! I'm the one who likes worms!"

But he just stood there grinding his teeth, tapping his fingers tensely on the tabletop.

Still scribbling notes about Patrick's project, the judges moved on to the next project—Liquids and Gases.

Patrick turned to Todd and forced him into slapping another high five. "You can come over and see my new computer any time," Patrick whispered confidently.

Todd forced a weak laugh. He turned away from Patrick—and found his sister glaring at him furiously from the other side of the table.

"How *could* you, Todd!" she demanded, spitting out the words, her hands pressed tightly at her waist. "How could you do that to Beth and me?"

"Easy," he replied, unable to keep a grin off his face.

"You *ruined* our project!" Regina cried.

"I know," Todd said, still grinning. "You deserved it."

Regina started to sputter.

The loudspeaker above their heads crackled on. "Ladies and gentlemen, we have a winner!" Mrs Sanger declared.

291

The huge gym grew silent. No one moved.

"The judges have a winner!" Mrs Sanger repeated, her voice booming off the tile walls. "The grand-prize winner of this year's Science Expo is . . ."

12

"The winner is . . ." Mrs Sanger announced, "Danny Fletcher and his Balloon Solar System!"

The audience on the benches was quiet for a moment, but then erupted in cheers and applause. Todd's classmates on the floor applauded, too.

Todd turned and caught the startled expression on Danny's face. Several kids rushed forward to congratulate Danny. The balloons bobbed behind Danny as he grinned and took a funny bow.

The gym erupted as everyone began to talk at once. Then the spectators made their way down from the benches and began wandering through the displays.

I don't *believe* this! Todd thought. Glancing at Patrick, he saw that Patrick felt the same way.

Danny flashed Todd a thumbs-up sign. Todd returned it, shaking his head.

He felt a hard shove on his shoulders.

"Hey—" he cried out angrily and spun round. "Are you still here?"

Regina glared at him angrily. "That's for ruining our project!" she shouted.

She shoved him again. "You apologize!" she demanded furiously.

He laughed. "No way!"

She growled at him and raised her fists. "Go eat worms!" she screamed.

Still laughing, he pulled off the wooden back of his worm house and lifted up a long, brown worm. He dangled it in front of his sister's face. "Here. Have some dessert."

With a furious cry, Regina completely lost all control.

She leaped at Todd, shoving him over backwards.

He cried out as he sprawled back—and hit the table hard.

Several kids let out startled screams as the enormous worm skyscraper tilted . . . tilted . . . tilted . . .

"No!" Patrick screamed. He reached out both hands to stop it.

And missed.

And the heavy wood-and-glass structure toppled on to the next table with a deafening crash of shattered glass.

"No!" a girl screamed. "That's Liquids and

294

Gases! Look out—it's Liquids and Gases!"

Dirt poured out of the broken skyscraper. Several worms came wriggling out on to the table.

As Todd pulled himself to his feet, wild screams filled the gym.

"Liquids and Gases!"

"What's that smoke?"

"What did they break? Did they break a window?"

"Liquids and Gases!"

Thick, white smoke poured up from a broken glass bottle under the fallen skyscraper.

"Everybody out!" someone yelled. "Everybody out! It's going to blow up!"

No one was hurt in the explosion.

Some strange gases escaped, and it smelled pretty weird in the gym for a while.

A lot of worms went flying across the room. And there was a lot of broken glass to be cleaned up.

But it was a minor explosion, Todd told his parents later. "Really. No big deal," he said. "I'm sure everyone will forget all about it in five or ten years."

A few days later, carrying a small, white box in both hands, Todd made his way down the basement stairs. He could hear the steady *plonk plonk* of ping-pong balls against bats.

Regina and Beth glanced up from their game as he entered the room. "Chinese food?" Beth asked, spotting the little box.

"No. Worms," Todd replied, crossing the room to his worm tank.

"Are you still into worms?" Beth demanded, twirling her ping-pong bat. "Even after what happened at the Science Expo?"

"It all got cleaned up," Todd snapped. "It was no big deal."

"Hah!" Regina cried scornfully.

Todd gazed at his sister in surprise. "Hey, are you talking to me again?" Regina was so furious, she hadn't said a word to him since the big disaster.

"No. I am not talking to you," Regina replied with a sneer. "I will never talk to you again."

"Give me a break!" Todd muttered. He opened the box and poured the new worms into the big glass aquarium where he stored his collection.

Plonk. Plonk. The girls returned to their game.

"You know, what happened at the Science Expo was no tragedy," Todd called to them. "Some people thought it was pretty funny." He sniggered.

"Some people are pretty *sick*," Beth muttered.

Regina slammed the ball hard. It sailed into the net. "You ruined everything," she accused Todd angrily. "You ruined the whole expo."

"And you ruined our project," Beth added, reaching for the ball. "You made us look like total jerks."

297

"So?" Todd replied, laughing.

The girls didn't laugh.

"I only did it because you sent Danny and me to that creepy old house," Todd told them. He used a small trowel to soften the dirt in the worm tank.

"Well, you wouldn't have won, anyway," Regina said, sneering. "Patrick's skyscraper made your puny house look like a baby's project."

"You're jealous of Patrick—aren't you, Todd?" Beth accused him.

"Jealous of that copycat?" Todd cried. "He doesn't know one end of a worm from another!"

The girls started their game again. Beth took a wild swing and sent the ball sailing across the room.

Todd caught it with his free hand. "Come here," he said. "I'll show you something cool."

"No way," Regina replied nastily.

"Just toss back the ball," Beth said, holding up her hand to catch it.

"Come here. This is really cool," Todd insisted, grinning.

He pulled a long worm out of the tank and held it up in the air. It wriggled and squirmed, trying to get free.

Regina and Beth didn't move away from the table. But he saw that they were watching him.

Todd set the long worm down on the table and picked up a pocket knife. "You watching?" With one quick motion, he sliced the worm in half.

"Yuck!" Beth cried, making a disgusted face.

"You're sick!" Regina declared. "You're really sick, Todd."

"Watch!" Todd instructed.

All three of them stared at the tabletop as the two worm halves wriggled off in different directions.

"See?" Todd cried, laughing. "Now there are *two* of them!"

"Sick. Really sick," his sister muttered.

"That's disgusting, Todd," Beth agreed, shaking her head.

"But wouldn't it be cool if people could do that?" Todd exclaimed. "You know. Your bottom half goes to school, and your top half stays at home and watches TV!"

"Hey! Look at that!" Regina cried suddenly. She pointed to the glass worm tank.

"Huh? What?" Todd demanded, lowering his eyes to the worms.

"Those worms—they were watching you!" Regina exclaimed. "See? They're sort of staring at you."

"Don't be stupid," Todd muttered. But he saw that Regina was right. Three of the worms had their heads raised out of the dirt and seemed to be staring up at him. "You have a weird imagination," Todd insisted.

"No. They were watching," Regina insisted excitedly. "I saw them watching you when you cut that worm in two."

"Worms can't see!" Todd told them. "They weren't watching me. That's stupid! That's—"

"But they *were*!" Regina cried.

"The worms are angry," Beth added, glancing at Regina. "The worms don't like to see their friend cut in half."

"Stop," Todd pleaded. "Just give me a break, okay?"

"The worms are going to get revenge, Todd," Regina said. "They saw what you did. Now they're planning their revenge."

Todd let out a scornful laugh. "You must think I'm as stupid as you are!" he declared. "There's no way I'm going to fall for that. No way I'm going to believe such a stupid idea."

Giggling to each other, Regina and Beth returned to their ping-pong game.

Todd dropped the two worm halves into the tank. To his surprise, four more worms had poked up out of the soft dirt. They were staring straight up at him.

Todd stared down at them, thinking about what Regina and Beth had said.

What a stupid idea, he thought. Those worms weren't watching me.

Or *were* they?

"Todd—rise and shine!"

Todd blinked his eyes open. He sat up slowly in bed and stretched his arms over his head.

"Rise and shine, Todd! Look alive!" his mother called from the foot of the stairs.

Why does she say the same thing every morning? he wondered. Always "Rise and shine, rise and shine!" Why can't she say, "Time to get up!" or, "Move 'em on out!" or something? Just for a little variety.

Grumpily, he pulled himself up and lowered his feet to the floor.

Why can't I have a clock radio like Regina? he asked himself. Then I could wake up to music instead of "Rise and shine!"

"Look alive up there!" Mrs Barstow called impatiently.

"I'm up! I'm up, Mum!" Todd shouted hoarsely down to her.

Bright sunlight poured in through the bedroom window. Squinting towards the window, he could see a patch of clear blue sky.

Nice day, he thought.

What day is it? he asked himself, standing up and stretching some more. Thursday? Yeah. Thursday.

Good, he thought. We have gym on Thursday. Maybe we'll play softball.

Gym was Todd's favourite class—especially on days they went outside.

His pyjama bottoms had become totally twisted. He straightened them as he made his way to the bathroom to brush his teeth.

Are we having the maths test today or tomorrow? he wondered, squinting at his sleepy face in the medicine cabinet mirror. I hope it's tomorrow. I forgot to study for it last night.

He stuck his tongue out at himself.

He could hear Regina downstairs, arguing about something with their mother. Regina liked to argue in the morning. It was the way she got her mind into gear.

She argued about what to wear. Or what she wanted for breakfast. One of her favourite arguments was whether or not it was too warm to wear a jacket.

Todd's mother never learned. She always argued back. So they had pretty noisy mornings.

Todd liked to sleep as long as possible. Then he

took his time getting dressed. That way, Regina had usually finished all her arguing by the time he came downstairs.

Thinking about the maths test, he brushed his teeth. Then he returned to his room and pulled on a clean pair of faded jeans and a navy blue T-shirt that came down nearly to his knees.

Regina and Mrs Barstow were still arguing as Todd entered the kitchen. Regina, her dark hair tied back in a single plait, sat at the table, finishing her breakfast. Their mother, dressed for work, stood on the other side of the table, a steaming cup of coffee in one hand.

"But I'm too hot in that jacket!" Regina was insisting.

"Then why not wear a sweatshirt?" their mother suggested patiently.

"I don't have any," Regina complained.

"You have a whole drawerful!" Mrs Barstow protested.

"But I don't like those!" Regina cried shrilly.

Todd grabbed his glass of orange juice off the table and gulped it down in one long swallow.

"Todd, sit down and have your breakfast," his mother ordered.

"Can't. I'm late," he said, wiping orange juice off his upper lip with one hand. "Got to go."

"But you haven't brushed your hair!" Mrs Barstow exclaimed.

304

Regina, chewing on a piece of rye toast, laughed. "How can you tell?"

Todd ignored her. "No need," he told his mother. "I'm wearing my Raiders cap." He glanced towards the hook on the hallway wall where he thought he had left it. Not there.

"I can't believe the school lets you wear your cap all day," Mrs Barstow murmured, refilling her coffee cup.

"They don't care," Todd told her.

"Only the real grunges wear caps," Regina reported.

"Is your brother a grunge?" their mother asked, raising her eyes over the white mug as she sipped coffee.

"Has anyone seen my Raiders cap?" Todd asked quickly, before Regina could answer.

"Isn't it on the hook?" Mrs Barstow asked, glancing towards the hall.

Todd shook his head. "Maybe I left it upstairs." He turned and hurried towards the front stairs.

"Come back and eat your cereal! It's getting soggy!" his mother called.

Grabbing on to the banister, Todd took the stairs two at a time. Standing in the doorway to his room, his eyes searched the bed. The top of the chest of drawers.

No cap.

He was halfway to the wardrobe when he

305

spotted it on the floor. I must have tossed it there before going to bed, he remembered.

Bending down, he picked up the cap and slid it down over his hair.

He knew at once that something was wrong.

Something felt funny.

As he bent the peak down the way he liked it, he felt something move in his hair.

Something wet.

It felt as if his hair had come to life and had started to crawl around under the cap.

Moving quickly to the mirror over the chest of drawers, Todd pulled the cap away—and stared in shock at the fat, brown worms wriggling through his hair.

Todd shook his head hard. A shudder of surprise.

One of the worms toppled from his hair and slid down his forehèad, dropping on to the chest of drawers.

"I don't believe this," Todd muttered out loud.

He tossed the cap to the floor. Then he reached up with both hands and carefully began untangling the worms from his hair.

"Regina!" he screamed. "Regina—you're going to pay for this!"

He pulled three worms off his head, then picked up the fourth from the chest of drawers. "Yuck." He made a disgusted face into the mirror. His hair was damp and sticky where the worms had crawled.

"Okay, Reggie! I'm coming!" he shouted as he bounded down the stairs, the worms dangling in one fist.

She glanced up casually from the table as Todd burst into the kitchen.

"Your cereal is really getting soggy," his mother said from the sink. "You'd better—" She stopped when she saw the worms in Todd's hand.

"Very funny, Regina!" Todd exclaimed angrily. He shoved the fistful of worms under his sister's nose.

"Yuck! Get away!" she shrieked.

"Todd—get those worms away from the table!" Mrs Barstow demanded sharply. "What's *wrong* with you? You know better than that!"

"Don't yell at *me*!" Todd screeched at his mother. "Yell at *her*!" He pointed furiously at his sister.

"Me?" Regina's eyes opened wide in innocence. "What did I do?"

Todd let out an angry groan and turned to face his mother. "She stuffed worms in my cap!" he exclaimed, shaking the worms in Mrs Barstow's face.

"Huh?" Regina cried furiously. "That's a *lie*!"

Todd and Regina began screaming accusations at each other.

Mrs Barstow stepped between them. "Quiet—please!" she demanded. "Please!"

"But—but—!" Todd sputtered.

"Todd, you're going to squeeze those poor

worms to death!" Mrs Barstow declared. "Go and put them away in the basement. Then take a deep breath, count to ten, and come back."

Todd grumbled under his breath. But he obediently headed down to the basement.

When he returned to the kitchen a minute later, Regina was still denying that she had loaded the cap with worms. She turned to Todd, a solemn expression on her face. "I swear, Todd," she said, "it wasn't me."

"Yeah. Sure," Todd muttered. "Then who else did it? Dad? Do you think Dad filled my cap with worms before he went to work?"

The idea was so ridiculous, it made all three of them laugh.

Mrs Barstow put her hands on Todd's shoulders and guided him into his seat at the table. "Cereal," she said softly. "Eat your cereal. You're going to be late."

"Leave my worms alone," Todd told his sister in a low voice. He pulled the chair in and picked up the spoon. "I mean it, Reggie. I hate your stupid jokes. And I don't like people messing with my worms."

Regina sighed wearily. "I don't mess with your disgusting worms," she shot back. "I told you—I didn't do it."

"Let's just drop it, okay?" Mrs Barstow pleaded. "Look at the clock."

"But why should she get away with that,

Mum?" Todd demanded. "Why should she be allowed to—"

"Because I didn't do it!" Regina interrupted.

"You *must* have done it!" Todd screamed.

"I think you did it yourself," Regina suggested with a sneer. "I think you stuffed worms in your own cap."

"Oh, that's good! That's good!" Todd cried sarcastically. "Why, Regina? Why would I do that?"

"To get me in trouble," Regina replied.

Todd gaped at her, speechless.

"You're *both* going to be in trouble if you don't drop this discussion—right now," their mother insisted.

"Okay. We'll drop it," Todd grumbled, glaring at his sister.

He dipped the spoon into the cereal. "Totally soggy," he muttered. "How I am supposed to—"

Regina's shrill scream cut off Todd's complaint.

He followed her horrified gaze down to his bowl—where he found a fat purple worm floating on top of the milk.

16

Todd tried to concentrate at school, but he kept thinking about the worms.

Of *course* it had to be Regina who had put the worms in his cap and in his cereal bowl.

But she had acted so shocked. And she said again and again that she didn't know anything about them.

Todd kept thinking about the afternoon in the basement. About cutting the worm in half. About the other worms watching him from their glass tank.

"They saw what you did," his sister had said in a low, frightened voice. "And now they're planning their revenge."

That's so stupid, Todd thought, pretending to read his social studies text.

So stupid.

But thinking about Regina's words gave him a chill.

And thinking about the worms waiting in his

311

cap, crawling so wetly through his hair, made Todd feel a little sick.

He told Danny all about it at lunch.

They sat across from each other in the noisy lunchroom. Danny unpacked his lunch from the brown paper lunch bag and examined the sandwich. "Ham and cheese again," he groaned. "Every day Mum gives me ham and cheese."

"Why don't you ask for something else?" Todd suggested.

"I don't like anything else," Danny replied, tearing open his bag of crisps.

Todd unpacked his lunch, too. But he left it untouched as he told Danny about the worms.

Danny laughed at first. "Your sister is such a pain," he said through a mouthful of crisps.

"I suppose you're right," Todd replied thoughtfully. "It's *got* to be Regina. But she acted so surprised. I mean, she *screamed* when she saw the worm floating in the cereal."

"She probably practised screaming all day yesterday," Danny said, chomping into his sandwich.

Todd unwrapped the tinfoil from his sandwich. Peanut butter and jam. "Yeah. Maybe," he said, frowning.

"Come on, Todd," Danny said, mustard dripping down his chin. "That worm tank of yours is really deep. The worms didn't crawl out all by

312

themselves. And they didn't crawl upstairs to your room and then find your hat and crawl inside."

"You're right. You're right," Todd said, still frowning thoughtfully. He pushed back his Raiders cap and scratched his brown hair. "But I just keep seeing those worms staring at me, and—"

"Worms don't have eyes!" Danny declared. "And they don't have faces. And, mainly, they don't have brains!"

Todd laughed. Danny was completely right, he realized.

The idea of worms planning to get their revenge was just ridiculous.

Feeling a lot better, he slid down in the chair and started his lunch. "Let's talk about something else," he said, taking a long drink from his carton of juice. He raised his peanut butter and jam sandwich to his mouth and took a big bite.

"Did you see Dawkins fall off his chair this morning?" Danny asked, sniggering.

Todd grinned. "Yeah. Miss Grant jumped so high, her head nearly hit the ceiling! I thought she was going to drop her teeth!"

"Luckily Dawkins landed on his head!" Danny exclaimed, wiping the mustard off his chin with the back of one hand. "Dawkins can't stay on a chair. No balance, or something. Every day he—"

Danny stopped when he saw the sick expression on Todd's face. "Hey, Todd—what's the matter?"

"Th-this peanut butter sandwich," Todd stammered. "It . . . tastes kind of strange."

"Huh?" Danny lowered his eyes to the half-eaten sandwich in Todd's hand.

Reluctantly, Todd pulled apart the two slices of bread.

Both boys moaned in disgust and let out hoarse gagging sounds as they saw the half-eaten purple worm curled up in the peanut butter.

"Have you seen my sister?" Todd asked a group of kids at the door that led out to the playground.

They all shook their heads no.

After angrily tossing away his lunch, Todd had run out of the lunchroom in search of Regina. He had to let her know that her stupid joke had gone too far.

Putting a worm in his peanut butter wasn't the least bit funny. It was *sick*.

As he ran through the halls, searching in each room for her, Todd could still taste the faintly sour flavour of the worm, could still feel its soft squishy body between his teeth.

It made his teeth itch. It made him feel itchy all over.

Regina, you're not getting away with this! he thought bitterly.

By the time he reached the end of the hallway, he felt so angry, he was seeing red.

He pushed past the group of kids, opened the

door, and burst outside. The bright afternoon sunlight made him lower his cap to shield his eyes.

He searched the playground for his sister.

Some kids from his class were playing a loud, frantic kickball game on the softball diamond. Jerry Dawkins and a few other guys called to Todd to join the game.

But he waved them off and kept running. He was in no mood for games.

Regina—where are you?

He circled the entire playground and teacher car park before he gave up. Then he slowly, unhappily, trudged back towards the school building.

His stomach growled and churned.

He could picture the worm half wriggling around inside him.

All around, kids were yelling and laughing and having fun.

They didn't eat worms for lunch, Todd thought bitterly. They don't have a mean, vicious sister who tries to ruin their lives.

He was nearly to the door, walking slowly, his head bowed, when he spotted Regina standing in the shade at the corner of the building.

He stopped and watched her. She was talking to someone. Then she started to laugh.

Keeping against the redbrick wall, Todd edged

a little closer. He could see two others in the shade with Regina.

Beth and Patrick.

All three of them were laughing now.

What was so funny?

Todd could feel the rage boiling up in him. As he crept closer, trying to hear what they were saying, he clenched his hands into tight, angry fists.

Pressing against the building, Todd stopped and listened.

Regina said something. He couldn't make out the words.

He took a step closer. Then one more.

And he heard Beth laugh and say, "So Todd doesn't know you're doing it?"

And then Patrick replied, "No. Todd doesn't know. He doesn't know I'm doing it."

Stunned, Todd jammed his back against the brick wall.

Patrick?

How can *Patrick* be doing it? Todd wondered. That's impossible! Unless . . .

Todd couldn't hold back any longer. He angrily stepped forward, feeling his face grow red-hot.

The three of them turned in surprise.

"So *you're* doing it?" Todd cried to Patrick. "You're giving my sister the worms?"

"Huh? Worms?" Patrick's mouth dropped open. He held a large sheet of paper in his hand. Todd saw him slip the sheet of paper behind his back.

"Yeah. Worms," Todd repeated, snarling the words. "I heard what you said, Patrick."

"Patrick isn't giving me worms," Regina broke in. "What is your problem, Todd? Why would I want worms?"

"That's where you're getting them!" Todd insisted. "I heard you! I heard the whole thing!"

The three of them exchanged bewildered glances.

"I'm not into worms any more," Patrick said. "I tossed all my worms into my dad's garden."

"Liar," Todd accused in a low voice.

"No. It's true. I helped him," Beth said.

"I got bored with them. I don't collect them any more," Patrick told him. "I'm into comic strips now."

"Huh? Comic strips?" Todd stared suspiciously at Patrick.

The two girls began to grin.

"Yeah. I'm drawing comic strips," Patrick said. "I'm a pretty good artist."

He's just trying to confuse me, Todd thought angrily.

"Patrick—give me a break," Todd muttered. "You're a really bad liar. I *heard* what you were saying, and—"

With a quick move, Todd reached out and grabbed the sheet of paper from behind Patrick's back.

"Hey—give that back!" Patrick reached for it. But Todd swung it out of his reach.

"Huh? It's a comic strip!" Todd exclaimed. He raised it closer to his face and started to read it.

THE ADVENTURES OF TODD THE WORM

That was the title in big, block, super-hero-type letters.

And in the first panel, there stood a smiling worm. With wavy brown hair. Wearing a silver-and-black Raiders cap.

"Todd the Worm?" Todd cried weakly, staring at the comic strip in disbelief.

The three of them burst out laughing.

"That's what we were laughing about," Regina told him, shaking her head. "Patrick can draw pretty well—can't he?"

Todd didn't reply. He scowled at the comic strip.

Todd the Worm. A worm in a Raiders cap.

Patrick thinks he's so funny, Todd thought bitterly. "Ha-ha. Remind me to laugh some-time," he murmured sarcastically. He handed the sheet of paper back to Patrick.

The bell on the side of the building rang loudly above their heads. Todd covered his ears. Every-one in the playground started running to the door.

Beth and Regina jogged ahead of Todd.

"So what about the worm in my sandwich?" he called to his sister, hurrying to catch up. He grabbed her by the shoulder and spun her around. "What about the worm?"

"Todd—let go!" She spun out of his grasp. "What worm? Are you still carrying on about breakfast?"

320

"No. Lunch," Todd shouted furiously. "You know what I'm talking about, Reggie. Don't pretend."

She shook her head. "No, I really don't, Todd." She turned to the door. "We're going to be late."

"You put the worm in my sandwich!" he screamed, his eyes locked on hers.

She made a disgusted face. "Yuck! In your sandwich?" She seemed really shocked. "That's disgusting!"

"Regina—"

"You didn't *eat* it, did you?" she asked, covering her mouth in horror.

"Uh . . . no. No way!" Todd lied.

"Ugh! I'm going to be sick!" Regina cried. She turned and, still covering her mouth, ran into the building.

Todd stared after her. She seemed totally shocked, he realized.

Is it possible that Regina didn't do it?

Is it possible?

But then, if Regina didn't do it—*what does that mean*?

"Aren't you sick of worms? Why are we digging up more worms?" Danny demanded.

Todd dug his shovel into the soft mud behind second base. "I need more," he murmured. He pulled up a long, brown one. It wriggled between his fingers. "Move the bucket over, Danny."

Danny obediently held the bucket closer. Todd dropped the worm into it and bent to dig up more. "My worms are all disappearing," he said softly, concentrating on his work. "They're escaping, I guess. So I need more."

"But they *can't* escape," Danny insisted.

Todd dropped a short, fat one into the bucket.

They both heard the rumbling sound at the same time.

The ground behind second base trembled.

Danny's eyes grew wide with fright. "Todd—another earthquake?"

Todd tilted his head as he listened. He dropped

322

the shovel and placed both hands flat on the ground. "It—it's shaking a little," he reported.

"We've got to go!" Danny cried, climbing to his feet. "We've got to tell someone."

"Nobody ever believes us," Todd replied, not moving from the ground. "And, look—the rest of the playground doesn't seem to be shaking at all."

The mud made a soft cracking sound as it trembled.

Todd jumped to his feet and grabbed the bucket.

"Maybe we should find another place to get worms," Danny suggested, backing away from the spot, his eyes on the shaking ground.

"But this is the best spot!" Todd replied.

"Maybe it's a sinkhole!" Danny declared as they hurried off the playground. "Did you see that sinkhole on the news? A big hole just opened up in somebody's back garden. And it grew bigger and bigger, and people fell in it and were swallowed up."

"Stop trying to scare me," Todd told his friend. "I've got enough problems without worrying about sinkholes!"

When he arrived at school on Friday morning, Todd found three worms wriggling around in his backpack. He calmly carried them out to the front of the school and deposited them in the dirt under the long hedge that lined the building.

I'm going to stay calm, he decided.

They're only worms, after all. And I like worms. I collect worms. I'm a worm expert.

He returned to the building, frowning fretfully.

If I'm such an expert, he asked himself, why can't I explain how the worms are following me everywhere?

When he took out his maths notebook an hour later, he found a mass of long purple worms crawling around near the binding and between the pages.

The kids sitting near him saw them and started pointing and screaming.

"Todd," Mr Hargrove, the maths teacher, said sternly, "I think we saw enough of your worms at the Science Expo. I know you're attached to them. But do you have to bring them to maths class?"

Everyone laughed. Todd could feel his face growing hot.

"Todd's saving them for lunch!" Danny exclaimed from two rows behind him.

Everyone laughed even louder.

Thanks a bunch, Danny, Todd thought angrily. He scooped the worms up, carried them to the window, and lowered them to the ground.

Later, in the lunchroom, Todd unwrapped his

sandwich carefully. Peanut butter and jam again.

Danny leaned across the table, staring hard at the sandwich.

"Go ahead. Open it," he murmured.

Todd hesitated, gripping the sandwich in both hands.

How many worms would be crawling through the peanut butter this time? Two? Three? *Ten?*

"Go ahead," Danny urged. "What are you waiting for?"

Todd took a deep breath and held it. Then he slowly pulled apart the two slices of bread.

"No worm!" Todd declared.

Both boys let out long sighs of relief.

Danny sank back into his seat and picked up what was left of his ham sandwich.

Todd didn't eat. He stared thoughtfully at the peanut butter covered with smears of black-currant jam. "They're going to drive me totally crazy," he muttered.

"What?" Danny asked with a mouthful of sandwich.

"Nothing," Todd replied. His head itched. He pulled off his cap and reached up to scratch it. He expected to find a worm in his hair. But there wasn't one.

Every time he opened his book bag, he expected to find worms. Every time he ate a meal, he expected to see a worm bobbing or wriggling or crawling or swimming through his food.

He was starting to imagine worms every-where. Everywhere.

Todd had dinner at Danny's that night. Danny's mother served fried chicken and mashed potatoes. Then she and Danny's father argued all through dinner about where to go on holiday, and whether or not they should save the money and buy a couch instead.

Danny seemed really embarrassed about his parents' loud arguing.

But Todd didn't mind at all. He was so happy to relax and eat and not worry about finding any long, purple worms on his plate or in his glass.

He and Danny went up to Danny's room and played video games for a few hours after dinner. Danny had a game called Worm Attack. Todd made him bury it at the back of the cupboard.

Danny's father drove Todd home at about ten. Todd's parents were already dressed for bed. "Your mum and I both had rough days," Mr Barstow explained. "We're hitting the sack early. You can stay up and watch TV or something if you want, Todd."

Todd didn't feel sleepy. So he went into the den and turned on the TV. He watched a *Star Trek* that he'd already seen.

He was yawning and feeling tired by the time the show finished at eleven. He turned off all the lights and made his way up to his room.

He realized he was feeling really good, really relaxed. I haven't thought about worms all night, he told himself happily.

He climbed out of his clothes, tossing them on to the floor, and pulled on his pyjamas. A warm, soft wind was fluttering the curtains at the window. He could see a pale half-moon in the black night-time sky.

Clicking off the bedside lamp, Todd pulled back his covers and slipped into bed.

He yawned loudly and shut his eyes.

Tomorrow is Saturday, he thought happily. No school.

He turned on to his stomach and buried his face in the pillow.

He felt something wet and warm wriggle against his cheek.

Then he felt something moving under his chest.

"Oh!" He jerked himself upright, pulling himself up with both hands.

A long, wet worm clung to the side of his face.

He reached up and pulled it off.

He jumped out of bed. It took a short while to find the bedside lamp in the darkness. Finally, he managed to click it on.

Blinking in the light, he saw a worm stuck to the front of his pyjama top. Three long, brown worms were crawling on his sheet. Two more were stretched out on the pillow.

"No! No! Stop!"

It took Todd a while to realize that the shrill screams were coming from *him*!

"I can't take it any more!" he shrieked, losing control.

He pulled the worm off his pyjama top and tossed it on to the bed beside the others.

"Regina! Regina—you've got to stop it! You've *got* to!" Todd screamed.

He spun round when he heard footsteps at the bedroom door.

"Mum!" Todd wailed. "Mum—look!" He pointed frantically to the worms crawling on his pillow and bedsheet.

Mrs Barstow raised both hands to her cheeks in surprise.

"Mum—you've got to stop Regina!" Todd pleaded. "You've got to stop her! Look what she did! Look what she put in my bed!"

Mrs Barstow moved quickly into the room and put an arm around Todd's trembling shoulders. "But Regina isn't here, Todd," she said gently.

"Huh?" He gaped at her in shock.

"Regina is at a sleepover at Beth's," his mother explained. "Regina isn't here!"

"We'll have to have a long discussion about this in the morning," Mrs Barstow said, her arm still around Todd's shoulders. "Maybe your worms are escaping from the tank somehow."

"Maybe," Todd replied thoughtfully.

His mother lowered her eyes to the bed. "Yuck. Take the worms back downstairs, Todd, and I'll change the sheets."

Todd obediently lifted the worms off the sheet and pillowcase. Two of them were mashed. But the rest were wriggling and squirming.

They're taking their revenge, Todd thought with a shudder as he carried them out of the room.

Regina was right.

The worms are paying me back.

The worms dangled from his hand as he carried them down to the basement. He dropped them into the tank. Then he leaned over it, staring down into the soft, wet dirt.

Most of the worms were below the surface. But a few crawled across the top.

"Hey," Todd called down to them, lowering his face over the top of the glass aquarium. "Hey, you lot—can you hear me?"

He had never talked to his worms before. And he felt very uncomfortable talking to them now.

But he was desperate.

"Listen, you lot, I'm really sorry," Todd said, speaking softly. He didn't want his voice to carry upstairs. If his mum or dad heard him talking to the worms, they'd know he was totally Looney Tunes.

"I'm really sorry about what happened," he told them. "I mean, about cutting that one in half. It will never happen again. I promise."

Leaning over the tank, he stared down into the dirt. The worms didn't seem to be paying any attention to him. Two of them were crawling against one of the glass walls. Another was burrowing into the dirt.

"So do you think you can stop following me around?" Todd continued, giving it one last try. "I mean, I don't want to get rid of you all. I've been collecting worms for a long time. But if you keep this up, well . . . you'll all have to go."

Todd lifted his head out and stood up straight. I can't believe I just did that, he thought.

Maybe I *am* totally nuts.

He glanced quickly around the basement, expecting Regina and his parents to pop out from behind the boiler, crying, "April fool!"

But no one else was down there. Luckily, no one had seen him actually pleading with the worms!

Feeling really foolish and confused, Todd trudged back up to his room. His mother was waiting for him in the hall outside his room. "What took so long?"

"Nothing," Todd muttered, feeling himself blush.

She swept a hand through his wavy, dark hair. "I never get to see your hair," she said, smiling. "It's always under that awful cap."

"Yeah. I know," Todd yawned.

"Go and change your pyjamas," she instructed him. "Those have worm juice all over them. I'll run you a hot bath."

"No. No bath," Todd said sharply. "I'm too tired."

"You don't want a bath after rolling around on worms?" Mrs Barstow demanded.

"Tomorrow. Okay?" he pleaded.

"Okay," she agreed. "But change your pyjamas. Good night."

Todd watched her make her way downstairs. Then he returned to his room and changed into clean pyjamas. He inspected the bed carefully, even though the sheets were new. Then he examined the pillow.

When he was certain there were no worms, he turned off the light and slipped into bed.

Lying on his back, he stared through the window at the pale half-moon—and thought about the worms.

Regina was sleeping over at Beth's—but the bed was full of worms.

How?

How were they wriggling into his backpack? Into his notebooks? Into his breakfast? His lunch?

The room began to whirl. Todd felt dizzy. So sleepy. So very sleepy . . .

But he couldn't stop puzzling about the worms. Such a mystery.

The night sky grew darker. The moon rose away from the window.

It's so late, Todd thought, and I can't get to sleep.

Maybe I do need a hot bath, he told himself, lowering his feet to the floor. Baths always relaxed him.

He crept silently out of his room and down the hall to the bathroom. He didn't want to wake his parents. Closing the bathroom door behind him, he clicked on the light. Then he turned on the water and filled the tub, making it nice and hot.

When the water was nearly up to the top, he

pulled off his pyjamas. Then he lowered himself into the steamy water. "Mmmmmm," he hummed aloud as he settled into it. The hot water felt so good, so soothing.

This was a good idea, he told himself, resting his head against the back of the tub. He smiled and shut his eyes. Just what I needed.

A soft splash made Todd open his eyes and glance at the tap. Had he forgotten to turn it off?

Another splash.

"Ohh." Todd let out a soft moan as a fat purple worm slid out of the tap and hit the water. "Oh, no!"

Splash.

Another worm dropped from the tap. Then two more. They hit the surface of the water and plunged to the tub bottom just past Todd's feet.

"Hey—!" He pulled his feet away and drew himself up to a sitting position. "What's going on?!"

As Todd stared in horror, brown and purple worms tumbled from the tap, three and four at a time, splashing into the bath. He raised his eyes to see more worms—sliding down the tile wall, plopping on to the water, on to his legs, on to his shoulders.

"No—!"

He struggled to climb out, trying to push himself to his feet with both hands.

But the bottom of the bath was covered with wriggling, swimming, slithering worms. And his hands kept slipping out from under him.

"Help—!"

Breathing hard, he managed to climb to his knees.

Worms clung to his back, his shoulders. He could feel them crawling over his hot, wet skin.

More worms tumbled down the wall. They seemed to be raining from the ceiling. More and more poured out of the tap.

They had turned the entire bath into a seething, wriggling sea of brown and purple.

"Help—somebody!" Todd shouted.

But the worms were pulling him now. Pulling him down.

He could feel their wet grasp, hundreds of tiny prickles, as they held him tightly and tugged him down, down, into the churning water.

They plopped on to his head. Crawled over his face. Dangled from his quivering shoulders.

Covered him. Covered him, and continued to rain down, to pour down, and pull him down with them, into the wriggling, dark sea of warm, wet worms.

"Please—help me!"

Todd struggled and squirmed. He twisted his body, trying to swing his arms free.

But the worms held on, forcing him down, pulling him into the slimy, brown water. And more worms rained down, curling and uncurling as they slid down the wall, dropped from the ceiling, and poured from the tap.

"Oh!"

He let out a startled cry as he tugged himself back to a sitting position. He thrashed his arms hard, sending a spray of water over the side of the bath.

He blinked. Once. Twice.

And the worms disappeared. All of them.

"Huh?" His mouth dropped open as he gazed into the bath. The ceiling light reflected in the clear water.

Hesitantly, he moved his toes. He splashed the water with both feet.

Clear. Perfectly clear and clean.

"Wow," Todd murmured, shaking his head. "Wow."

The wriggling, tumbling worms lingered in his mind. Despite the heat of the bathwater, a cold shiver ran down his body.

He climbed quickly out of the bath and wrapped a large, green bath towel around himself.

A dream. It had all been a disgusting dream.

He had fallen asleep in the bath and had dreamed up all of the worms.

He shivered again. He still felt shaky. He could still feel the itchy pinpricks all over his body.

Drying himself quickly, he let the towel slip to the floor and pulled on his pyjamas. Then, as he hurried back to his room, eager to climb under the covers—he had an idea.

He had an idea about how to solve the worm mystery.

It was so simple, he realized. Such a simple plan.

But it would tell him once and for all how the worms were escaping from their tank and getting into his things.

"Yes!" he cried in an excited whisper. "Yes!"

Finally, he had a plan. He knew exactly what to do.

It will have to wait till Sunday night, he told himself, climbing into bed and pulling up the blankets. But I'll be ready then.

Ready for anything.

Thinking about his plan, Todd fell asleep with a smile on his face.

The weekend passed slowly. Todd and Danny went to a film on Saturday. It was a comedy about space aliens trying to run a car wash. The aliens kept getting confused and washing themselves instead of cars. In the end, they blew up the whole planet.

Danny thought it was very funny. Todd thought it was stupid, but funny.

On Sunday, Regina came home from Beth's. The whole family went on a trip to visit some cousins.

"It was a no-worms weekend," Todd told Danny over the phone after dinner on Sunday evening.

"Excellent!" Danny replied enthusiastically.

"Not a single worm," Todd told him, twisting the phone cord around his wrist.

"So are you going ahead with your plan?" Danny demanded.

"Yeah. Sure," Todd said. "I have to. They just took the weekend off. For sure. Tomorrow is school. That means more worms in my backpack, in my books, in my lunch."

"Yuck," Danny murmured on the other end of the line.

"I've got to solve the mystery," Todd told him. "I've *got* to."

"Well, good luck," Danny said. "I'll meet you tomorrow morning. Outside Miss Grant's class, okay? Get there early so you can tell me how it went."

"Okay," Todd replied. "See you tomorrow." As he hung up the phone, he felt excited and nervous and eager and frightened, all at the same time.

He tried playing a Nintendo football game to pass the time. But he was so excited and nervous, he kept using the wrong fingers on the controls and the machine beat him easily.

Then he paced back and forth in his room, watching the clock slowly slide from number to number.

At ten-thirty, he and Regina said good night to their parents and returned to their rooms. Todd changed into his pyjamas, turned out the lights, then sat on the edge of his bed, waiting.

Waiting for his parents to go to bed.

He heard their door close at eleven-fifteen. Then he waited another fifteen minutes, sitting tensely in the dark, listening to the soft creaks and groans of the house, listening to the heavy silence.

A little after eleven-thirty, Todd climbed off his bed and tiptoed silently out of his room.

It's time, he told himself, creeping down the dark hall to the stairs. Time to get to the bottom of this.

Time to solve the mystery of the worms.

The basement stairs creaked loudly under Todd's bare feet. But there was nothing he could do about that.

He tried to move as silently as a mouse. He didn't want to alert anyone in his family that he was awake. He grabbed the wall and caught his balance as he started to stumble on the basement steps.

Taking a deep breath, he stopped and listened. Had anyone heard him?

Silence.

The wooden steps were steep and rickety. But Todd couldn't turn on the lights. He didn't want anyone to see him.

Not even the worms.

A pale square of light spread across the basement floor, moonlight pouring through the narrow window up near the basement ceiling. Todd stepped around the light, keeping in the dark shadows.

His heart pounded as he made his way slowly, carefully across the room. "Ow!" He let out a whispered cry as he banged his waist into the corner of the ping-pong table. He quickly covered his mouth before he could cry out again.

The pain slowly faded. Rubbing his side, Todd picked up a tall stool and carried it over to one of the concrete beams that rose from floor to ceiling.

He set the stool down slowly, carefully. Gazing around the beam, he could see the worm tank on its table. The glass tank reflected the glow of the moonlight that invaded the dark basement.

Todd lifted himself silently on to the stool. Hidden behind the square concrete beam, he could watch the worms—but they couldn't see him.

He gripped his hands around the beam and steadied himself on the tall stool. Glancing up, he saw the high window, filled with moonlight, glow like silver. The light cast eerie shadows over the entire basement.

Todd forced his breathing to slow to normal.

Got to take it easy. It may be a long wait, he told himself. I may be sitting here, watching the worm tank all night.

What did he expect to see?

He wasn't sure. But he knew something would

happen. Something would happen to explain the mystery of the worms to him.

Leaning against the beam, Todd stared at the glass aquarium tank. Were the worms plotting and planning inside? Were they deciding which ones of them would crawl upstairs and climb into Todd's things?

Todd suddenly imagined a different story. Glancing back at the silvery basement window, he imagined it opening. He imagined a dark figure sliding into the basement. Patrick. He imagined Patrick lowering himself on to the basement floor, then crossing the room to the worm tank.

He imagined Patrick pulling up worms from the tank and sneaking upstairs with them. Todd could see Patrick grinning as he dropped the worms into Todd's backpack, slipped one into the cornflakes box, hid one in Todd's trainer.

It's possible, Todd told himself, turning his attention back to the worms. It isn't a totally crazy idea. It isn't as crazy an idea as a bunch of worms planning their revenge . . .

He yawned, covering his mouth so the worms wouldn't hear.

How long will I have to sit here? he wondered. He felt a chill at the back of his neck. It was creepy down here in the dark.

What were those soft skittering sounds?

Mice?

He didn't have long to think about them. A loud *creak* behind him made Todd gasp.

He gripped the concrete beam.

The stairs began to groan.

He heard the slow thud of footsteps. Footsteps growing louder, moving down the stairs.

Todd lowered his feet to the floor. He pressed himself tightly behind the beam, trying to hide.

The stairs creaked and groaned.

The *thud* of footsteps stopped at the bottom of the steps. Todd squinted hard into the darkness.

Who was it? Who was sneaking down to the basement?

Who was sneaking down to the worm tank? Who?

Todd gasped as the ceiling lights flickered on. It took a second or two for his eyes to adjust to the bright fluorescent light.

Then he saw the figure standing at the light switch.

"*Dad!*" Todd cried.

Mr Barstow jumped in surprise. He had a yellow bathrobe slung loosely around him. He carried one of Todd's baseball bats in both hands, raised waist high.

"Dad—what are *you* doing down here?" Todd cried shrilly.

Todd's father lowered the baseball bat. His mouth dropped open as he squinted across the room at Todd. "What are *you* doing down here?" he demanded.

"I'm . . . uh . . . watching the worms," Todd confessed.

Mr Barstow let the bat drop to the floor. It clanked noisily at his feet. He made his way quickly over to Todd, carefully stepping around the ping-pong table.

"I heard the basement steps creaking," he told Todd. "I heard a crash down here, someone banging into the ping-pong table. I—I thought it was a burglar. So I grabbed the bat and came down to investigate."

"It's just me, Dad," Todd said. "I had to find out how my worms are getting into my stuff. So I decided to watch them all night and see if—"

"I've had it with those worms!" Mr Barstow exclaimed angrily.

"But, Dad—" Todd protested.

"What's going on down there? Are you okay?" Mrs Barstow called from the top of the stairs.

"Everything's okay, dear!" Todd's father called. "It's just more worm trouble."

"Those disgusting worms again? Come up here and get back to bed," Mrs Barstow ordered. Todd could hear her padding back to her room.

"Those worms are out of here tomorrow," Mr Barstow said sternly, tightening the belt of his yellow robe.

"What?" Todd cried. "Dad, please—"

"Enough is enough, Todd. I don't understand what's been going on with your worms," his father said, frowning, resting his hands on his waist. "But I can't have you scaring everyone in the house, sneaking around in the middle of the night, sitting in the dark, staring at a tank of worms instead of getting your sleep."

"But—but—" Todd sputtered.

Mr Barstow shook his head. "My mind is made up. No discussion. The worms go. Tomorrow afternoon, take them outside and dump them all in the garden."

"But, Dad—"

Mr Barstow raised a hand for silence. "I mean it. In the garden. Tomorrow afternoon. I'm sure you can find something better to collect than worms."

He placed both hands on Todd's shoulders and marched him towards the stairs.

Todd sighed unhappily, but didn't say any more. He knew better than to argue with his father. When his dad made up his mind about something, he could be very stubborn.

Todd climbed the rest of the way to his room in silence, feeling angry and disappointed.

As he dropped on to his bed and jerked up the covers, he grumbled to himself about the most disappointing thing of all—he hadn't solved the mystery.

All that planning. All that sneaking around.

He'd had such high hopes for getting to the bottom of it once and for all.

But, no.

Not only was he about to lose all of his worms,

347

but now he would *never* know how the worms got into his things.

I don't *care* about those stupid worms! he told himself. I don't *care* that I have to throw them all away!

All I really care about is solving the mystery!

Angry and frustrated, Todd turned and started to punch his pillow. Hard. With both fists. Again. Again.

He didn't realize that the whole mystery would be solved—accidentally—just a few hours later.

It rained the next morning. Todd didn't even notice as he walked slowly to school. His thoughts were darker than the storm clouds over his head.

He dropped his jacket in his locker and pulled out his Trapper-Keeper. Stuffing it into his rain-drenched backpack, he spotted Danny.

As planned, Danny was waiting outside the classroom door. Waiting to hear how Todd had solved the worm mystery.

Well, I guess Danny will just have to be disappointed, too, Todd thought glumly. He straightened his Raiders cap and, hoisting his wet backpack on to his shoulders, made his way across the hall to his friend.

Danny's red hair was soaked and matted down on his head. It looked more like a helmet than hair.

Todd pushed his way through a group of laughing, shouting kids, all shaking rainwater off themselves, puddles on the hall floor at their feet.

"So? How'd it go?" Danny asked eagerly as Todd stepped up to him.

Todd started to tell his friend the bad news— but he stopped when he heard a voice he instantly recognized.

Regina!

Around the corner, out of view of the two boys, Regina and Beth were sharing a good laugh.

"So he has to dump out all those disgusting worms today!" Regina was gleefully telling Beth. "Isn't that great?"

"Fantastic!" Beth declared.

Both girls laughed.

"Todd is such an idiot!" Beth exclaimed. "Did he really think the worms were crawling up-stairs on their own? Did he really think they were coming to get him?"

"Yeah. I think he did!" Regina said through her scornful laughter.

Around the corner from the two girls, Danny and Todd stood listening in shock. Neither of them moved a muscle. Todd's mouth had dropped open. He could feel his face growing red-hot.

"So today's the last day?" Beth was saying. "Did you put any worms in his stuff today?"

"Only two," Regina replied. "Mum gave him a thermos of hot vegetable soup since it's such a nasty day. I dropped one in the thermos. And I slipped one into his jacket pocket. He's on his way to school. He probably stuck his hand in and found my little surprise."

Both girls laughed again.

"And he never guessed it was you the whole time?" Beth asked Regina.

"He guessed," Regina replied. "But I'm such a good actress. I acted shocked and disgusted. Pretty soon, he didn't know *what* to think!"

They laughed some more. Then Todd heard them head the other way down the hall.

He turned to find Danny staring at him. "Todd—do you *believe* it? It was your sister the whole time!"

"I knew it," Todd lied, trying to sound casual. "I knew it was Regina."

"Well, what are you going to do?" Danny demanded, still staring at Todd.

"Get revenge, of course," Todd replied quickly.

"Revenge? How?" his friend asked.

"I'm not sure," Todd told him. "I just know it's going to take a *lot* of worms!"

The rain stopped after lunch. The heavy, dark clouds drifted away, and bright sunshine poured down from a clear blue sky.

Todd eagerly watched the weather change through the classroom windows. The sunshine filled him with hope.

This means the worms will be coming up from the ground, he thought happily. Dozens and dozens of worms.

He was desperate to get out and collect them. He was going to need a ton of worms to pay his sister back for her mean joke.

Unfortunately, just before school let out, he and Danny were caught having a glue fight during art class. Miss Travianti, the art teacher, made them both stay after school and clean up all the paintbrushes.

It was nearly four o'clock when Todd led the way to his favourite worm-collecting spot behind second base of the softball diamond. The playground was deserted. There were no other kids in sight.

Todd and Danny both carried empty coffee jars they had borrowed from the art room. Without saying a word, they bent down and set to work, pulling up long brown and purple worms, and dropping them into the jars.

"How many do we need?" Danny asked, poking in the soft mud till he found a big wet one.

"As many as we can get," Todd replied. He still hadn't figured out exactly what he was going to do to Regina. He just knew it was going to be totally amazing. And disgusting.

"You really should pay Beth back, too," Danny suggested. He dug a hole with his chubby hand and discovered three big worms tangled together.

"Yeah. You're right," Todd agreed. "We'll save some for Beth."

Todd stood up and pulled off his jacket. Even though it was late afternoon, the sun still beamed down. He was already sweating.

"Look at this one!" Danny declared. He held up a stubby pink worm.

"It's just a baby," Todd said. "Toss it in the jar, anyway. I need as many as I can get. Big or little."

Danny dropped the stubby pink worm in with the others.

353

Todd pulled up a really long one. He carefully brushed clumps of mud off it before dropping it in the jar. "The rain always brings up the really big ones," he told Danny.

The ground rumbled.

At first Todd didn't notice.

"Did you feel that?" Danny asked.

"Feel what?"

The ground shook again.

Todd heard a low rumbling sound, like distant thunder.

"Hey—!" Danny cried, alarmed. He stopped digging.

"That always happens," Todd told him. "No big deal. Keep digging."

Danny dug his hand back into the mud. But he jerked it out quickly when the ground shook again, harder this time. "Hey—why is this happening again?" he cried.

"I told you. It's nothing," Todd insisted.

But then a loud roar made them both cry out.

The entire playground seemed to tremble. The roar grew louder, closer.

The ground shook. Then both boys heard a cracking sound.

Todd started to his feet. But the ground shook so hard, he tumbled back down to his knees.

Craaaaaack.

"Oh, no!" Danny cried.

354

They both saw the dirt pull apart between them. It looked like a dark wound opening up.

Another rumble. The ground quivered and shook. The mud split open. Wider.

Wider.

And something poked up from under the ground.

At first, Todd thought it was a tree trunk.

It was dark brown like a tree trunk. And round like a tree trunk.

But it was moving too fast to be a tree, rising up from the opening in the mud.

And as the ground shook and the rumbling rose to a roar, Todd and Danny both realized that they were gaping in horror at a giant *worm*.

A worm as thick as a tree trunk.

Up, up it stretched, up from the mud, darting and dipping its enormous head.

Todd uttered a shriek of terror, and turned to run.

But his feet slipped on the wet, quivering mud. He fell forward, landing hard on his knees and elbows.

And before he could pull himself up, the enormous worm swung around him, swung around his waist, circled him, pulled itself tight.

"Ohhh!" he uttered a cry of panic.

A crazy thought burst into Todd's head: *This*

355

is the mother worm. She's come up to protect her babies.

And then another crazy thought: *The worms are really getting their revenge this time!*

And then he had no more time for crazy thoughts. Or any other kinds of thoughts.

Because the enormous worm was tightening itself around Todd's waist, choking off his breath, choking him, choking him.

Pulling him. Tugging him down into the mud, down into its cavernous hole.

He tried to call for help.

But no sound came out of his mouth.

He couldn't yell. He couldn't breathe.

The huge, wet worm was crushing him, crushing him as it pulled him down.

And then a dark shadow rolled over Todd. And everything went black.

Danny grabbed Todd's feet and tried to pull him free.

But the worm had wrapped itself around Todd's waist like a tight belt. Danny pulled Todd's ankles. Pulled hard.

But he couldn't free his friend.

And now the worm was disappearing back into the gaping hole in the mud, and taking Todd down with him.

And suddenly they were all covered in shadow.

"Huh?" Danny let out a startled gasp.

And raised his eyes to see what caused the shadow.

And saw the enormous robin bouncing along over the grass.

"Hey!" he frantically called out. "Regina! Beth!"

They were carrying the big papier-mâché bird home from school. He couldn't see their faces.

They were hidden on the other side of the enormous robin.

"Regina! Help us!"

And then the bird's shadow rolled over Danny and Todd.

And the worm jerked straight up. And began to tremble.

Did it see the shadow of the bird?

It jerked straight up—and let go of Todd.

Todd slid to the ground. And the quivering worm began to lower itself. Instantly, with a sickening sucking sound, it dived back into the mud.

Gasping for breath, Todd scrambled away on all fours.

The worm—it thinks Christopher Robin is a real bird! he realized.

When he glanced back, the worm had vanished back under the ground.

"Regina! Beth!" Todd and Danny shouted together.

The two girls slowly lowered their science project to the ground. "What do you want? What are you two doing here?" Regina demanded, poking her head around from the other side of the enormous robin.

"Did you see it?" Todd cried breathlessly. "Did you see the worm?"

"It was so huge!" Danny added, pulling Todd to his feet. "It was as tall as a building!"

358

"Ha-ha," Beth said sarcastically. "You guys must think we're really stupid."

"No way we're going to believe you caught a giant worm!" Regina added, shaking her head.

"You didn't see it?" Todd cried weakly. "You really didn't see it?"

"We're not making it up!" Danny shouted angrily. "It grabbed Todd. It was huge and brown and slimy! It was pulling Todd down."

"Give us a break," Beth groaned.

"Go eat worms," Regina said.

They hoisted up their giant robin and continued their slow trek towards the street.

Todd watched the bird's wide shadow roll over the grass. The shadow that had saved his life.

Then he turned to Danny with a weary shrug. "Might as well go home," he said softly. "I'm not sure I believe it myself."

Todd tossed all of his worms into the garden that afternoon. He told everyone he never wanted to see a worm again.

When Danny came over to Todd's house a few weeks later, he found Todd down in the basement, busy with a new hobby. "What are you doing?" Danny asked.

Todd's eyes remained on the fluttering

359

creature inside the glass jar on the worktable. "I'm chloroforming this butterfly," he told his friend.

"Huh? What do you mean?" Danny asked.

"I dipped a wad of cotton in chloroform and dropped it into the jar. It will kill the butterfly. Watch."

When the gold-and-black butterfly stopped fluttering, Todd carefully opened the jar. He lifted the butterfly out with long tweezers and gently spread its wings. Then he hung it on a board by sticking a long pin through its middle.

"You're collecting butterflies now?" Danny asked in surprise.

Todd nodded. "Butterflies are so gentle, so pretty," he said, concentrating on his work.

"Todd has changed a lot," Regina announced, appearing at the bottom of the stairs. "He isn't into *disgusting* any more. Now he's into things that are soft and beautiful."

"Let me show you some of my most beautiful butterfly specimens," Todd told Danny. "I have a few monarchs that will knock your eyes out."

Everyone was happy about Todd's new hobby. Especially Regina. There were no more cruel practical jokes played in the Barstow house.

Then, one night, Todd gazed up from his

worktable—and uttered a horrified cry as he saw a big creature fluttering towards him.

An enormous butterfly.

As big as a bedsheet!

Carrying an enormous silver pin.

"What are you going to *do*?" Todd cried.